Power Plays
Alexis Snipperdoom

JD Broyhill

ARCHWAY
PUBLISHING

Copyright © 2019 JD Broyhill.

All rights reserved. No part of this book may be used or reproduced by any means, graphic, electronic, or mechanical, including photocopying, recording, taping or by any information storage retrieval system without the written permission of the author except in the case of brief quotations embodied in critical articles and reviews.

This is a work of fiction. All of the characters, names, incidents, organizations, and dialogue in this novel are either the products of the author's imagination or are used fictitiously.

Archway Publishing books may be ordered through booksellers or by contacting:

Archway Publishing
1663 Liberty Drive
Bloomington, IN 47403
www.archwaypublishing.com
1 (888) 242-5904

Because of the dynamic nature of the Internet, any web addresses or links contained in this book may have changed since publication and may no longer be valid. The views expressed in this work are solely those of the author and do not necessarily reflect the views of the publisher, and the publisher hereby disclaims any responsibility for them.

Any people depicted in stock imagery provided by Getty Images are models, and such images are being used for illustrative purposes only. Certain stock imagery © Getty Images.

ISBN: 978-1-4808-7601-9 (sc)
ISBN: 978-1-4808-7600-2 (hc)
ISBN: 978-1-4808-7602-6 (e)

Library of Congress Control Number: 2019904484

Print information available on the last page.

Archway Publishing rev. date: 04/25/2019

To James, Jeremy, and Stephen - You are the
fire behind my words and inspiration!
To Rick - it never would have happened without you.
I am Alexis!

'Sometimes it is best to be Queen…. the power is wonderful!'

~Alexis Snipperdoom

Contents

The Beginning xi

chapter 1	Power Play	1
chapter 2	Enforcing Power	11
chapter 3	Kidnapped!	22
chapter 4	Revelations and Betrayal	38
chapter 5	New Beginnings	54
chapter 6	Revenge!	65
chapter 7	Unknown	73
chapter 8	Returning	82
chapter 9	Unexpected Surprises	94
chapter 10	The Calm before the Storm	99
chapter 11	Disclosures	113
chapter 12	Confrontations	124
chapter 13	Getting Even	134

The Beginning

"The weekly witches meeting has to be postponed. High Council Leader Grand Witch Alexis Snipperdoom has just given birth to her first child - it is a girl! We must visit at once and perform the Ritual of Newcome."

"Who will make the necessary announcement to the rest of the council? We must pass on this information immediately; we have all waited for such an occasion for a long time. Yes, our first Grand Princess of Witches. This is something new and historic. Surely, now all others will follow our way."

"Agreed!"

"We will make the announcement immediately. We must then visit Grand Witch Alexis to meet our future leader, the Princess Witch. What is the child's name? What are we to call her?"

"Her name is Lilah, Grand Princess of Witches of the Lunar Council."

chapter 1

Power Play

Alexis sprawled on her bed like a Queen. Yes, she was a Queen - Queen of Witches. This was something new for the council and the realm of Alstromia. At the beginning of the new solar year, she had been elected Queen of Witches to the Lunar Council. This new title would surely become an important new step in making Alstromia more powerful. Never, had there been such a change in leadership. The leadership had been taken away from a Warlock and given to a Witch!

The leadership change had been Alexis's idea. She desperately wanted to change history. She wanted to make history. She needed power and felt witchcraft was not enough. She truly was the most selfish of all witches and was known throughout her council as one with a cold heart. Many loved her evil ways; others despised her. Either way, Alexis did not care. She was aware of her reputation and planned to use it to her advantage.

The Queen of Witches had just given birth to her first child, a stunning baby girl. She would be the new Princess and future leader of all witches of Alstromia. Alexis and Armbruster, her husband, were very excited about the arrival of their heir. Armbruster, the head Chief of Warlocks, had fallen in love with Alexis the first time he met her at the Annual Meeting of Power. They were married within a month of meeting and made the birth announcement of their first child a year and a half later. They were a powerful team and many feared their leadership, while others respected them.

Alexis rolled onto her side as Armbruster walked into her chamber to hand her Lilah, the little, pink-faced Princess sleeping in his arms.

"She is beautiful, isn't she?" asked Alexis with a smirk. "Do you think she looks at all like me? She will be Queen one day, you know! She should and must look regal!"

"Oh Alexis, she is just a child. Look at her. She is perfect in every way. She is such a blessing to us and the entire council. Why do you worry so? She will be Queen one day and will be powerful. It does not matter what the child will look like. She will be a great leader, just like you. She will be strong and beautiful. Give her a chance. She will be our future leader and you will teach her well." Armbruster frowned as he looked at Alexis, as she rolled her big, green eyes at him. She was obviously not pleased with his comments and never hid her displeasure.

"Armbruster, you are too soft. Some days, I simply cannot understand your whining and attitude. She will be a leader one day. The leader of a new era. I know, without a doubt, she will be superior. I can only hope she will not be soft like you. You used to be such a powerful and respected Warlock. Now, sadly, you are this soft Warlock who only speaks of peace and hope. I hope she has the heart of steel that I possess. I find weakness a downfall and I simply will not allow that!" She sat up in bed and put out her arms so Armbruster could hand her the child. Alexis cradled her in her arms and smiled.

"Why do you talk like that, Alexis? You have changed my dear. I cannot comprehend what you are doing. You used to be so sweet and kind. What has made you so stoic and cold?" Armbruster was less than pleased with Alexis and her attitude. He had noticed many changes in her, none of them endearing. He feared her new position was going to her head and she was taking everything too seriously. She needed to calm down, allow the rest of the council to do their jobs, and stop worrying about making so many changes at once.

She laid the child on the bed and stood up. She walked over to Armbruster and stood in front of him. She lifted her long finger and pointed it right in his face, almost touching his nose.

"I am not cold. This council wants to make us witches something sweet and kind. We were never meant to be sweet and kind. We need to be feared; we need to maintain control over others! This is why I am Queen. Sometimes it is best to be Queen…the power is wonderful! This is why I am here. Anything else is just a waste of time. For generations, we have tried to blend into the real world. Enough! Let's make a stand and show our power."

She turned and walked back to the bed to pick up Lilah. Her anger softened as she looked into the eyes of her baby. The baby truly was the most stunning girl. She had a full head of black curls and big, pouty pink lips. Her unique eye color was a shade of a gray-lavender. Lilah had adorable little, chubby cheeks. Everything about the baby was regal and unique. Alexis knew she had produced the most gorgeous heir and was highly pleased with herself.

"You are boring me, Armbruster. You are not the man I met," Alexis announced with a frown on her face. Though Armbruster's physique was quite intimidating at times, she was not impressed. Yes, he was tall and handsome. Some, might even describe him as quite a catch. On occasion, some of the other women eyed him with pure lust. He stood tall, well over six feet, muscular and toned with broad shoulders. He had dark blue eyes, bushy but well-groomed eyebrows, long, strong arms and an incredible smile. He carried himself with confidence, the one quality Alexis liked more than others.

Armbruster shook his head in disgust. He did not know what was happening to his wife and the love of his life. "Darling, I feel you must rest. I think you are too exhausted to vent such energy.

I shall leave you and Lilah alone. The council is on their way to perform the Ritual of Newcome. Please, be properly dressed for it. I will not tolerate any more nonsense from you today."

Having said what was on his mind, he turned and walked out of the chamber. He headed down the corridor shaking his head, walking toward Council Hall. His mind ever wondering why she had changed. He worried child birth had changed her. Maybe she was ill? He grunted to himself as he walked on.

Enraged, Alexis placed Lilah on the bed and yelled for Carmin, Lilah's personal attendant. Who did Armbruster think he was talking to her like that? True, she had become Queen because of him, but by no means was he her equal. Why did he think for one second, he was so special that he could speak to her like that? Just wait, she would show him! She would show the council and the entire globe she was in charge!

Carmin ran straight to the royal chamber of the Queen. She knew better than to take her time, it would only result in trouble. She gently knocked on the door and walked into the room. There, she saw the Queen enraged by the window. Alexis turned to her and pointed to the bed.

"Get Lilah ready, I do not want to be late. Have her dressed and get her to the Hall immediately. Do you understand?" Alexis glared at Carmin.

"Yes, I understand Your Majesty. I will do so immediately." She gently picked up the child and left the room. She walked down to the next chamber, Lilah's room, and placed the Princess in her white crib. The bottom of the crib was padded with Pink Fluff, a soft and light material found growing on Trimbers, on the Enchanted Wall. Trimbers resembled trees on Earth but were found exclusively on Alstromia, a planet a blink away from Earth, inhabited only by witches. The planet remained untouched by humans and not visible to the human eye.

Carmin walked over to the wall closet and opened the massive, white doors. Inside hung a variety of gorgeous gowns handspun by the best and most-talented witches. Alexis had commissioned the best weavers to make the gowns when she found out she would be having a child. Carmin stretched out her arm and reached for a gown encased in a clear wrap. It was light purple with tiny, pink crystals. It was simply stunning. Next, she opened a drawer and pulled out matching shoes. She smiled as she looked at the sparkling tiara next to the shoes. Carmin beamed with delight as she changed Lilah's clothes and placed the soft tiara on her head.

Trumpets blared in the background, announcing the arrival of other council members and visitors. Carmin knew she had to hurry to take the child to the Hall. She placed the child in her silver Narry, an egg-shaped floating carriage. She walked down the hall with the Narry and the resting child, humming and grinning the entire way to the hall.

Meanwhile, in Council Hall, there was a lot of chatter surrounding the arrival of the new Princess and the grand announcement Armbruster and Queen Alexis were about to make.

Several warlocks helped other witches find their chairs.

In the background, a large stage held two massive chairs and a silver mini throne intended to hold the Narry to display the child to the Council. Three wide, glistening steps led up to the stage. Behind the stage, the view was spectacular. A massive, open window showcased the beautiful Valley of Grandu below. Trimbers lined the river of Miccay, which flowed softly with its usual dark gray water. Little huts of commoners lined the embankment. Further upstream, you could see the magnificent City of Miccay. It was where most council members resided.

The secure Palace of Snipperdoom sat up high in the hills, surrounded by large Trimbers, only accessible by flying Torrins, a horse-like animal. At first glance, these majestic beings seem to radiate an iridescent glow from their predominantly gold bodies. Up close, their clear, crystal eyes resembled flawless diamonds.

Torrins, anxious by nature, flailing their shiny, sleek, black wings and manes when in flight, looked magical. Under the right conditions, as the moonlight struck their fur, a mesmerizing purple glow emanated from them. Torrins, wild and untamed, usually required immense training. However, their keeper and trainer, Collan, was a very gifted commoner, hand selected by Alexis. He had a natural way with Torrins. Collan easily gained their trust and was able to tame the beasts quickly, without much effort.

Torrins tails showcased giant pearls from the Sea of Miccay, found off the city to the east. These regal creatures were housed adjacent to the Palace grounds in an enormous stable. Approaching the stable, you could see it was constructed of Trimbers, gray and black, with large, oval windows to accommodate the Torrin's heads. The tall doors, made of Ozar, a metal, strong enough to contain the feisty Torrins, granted entrance. Once inside, you were greeted by two tall and very wide rows of stalls. This building housed up to 80 Torrins. Alexis allowed the Torrins to be used to bring visitors to her Palace, though their primary purpose was transportation for her Security Command Team.

"Attention, council members. Please find a seat and be quiet. The Queen is about to enter the Hall. Please pick up the scrolls on your seat to acquaint yourself with the OOE (order of events)," stated Yarlen, the Second in Command of Warlocks. He was an elderly Warlock with fluffy, gray hair, pulled back into a long ponytail. He wore the robe of Warlock Command in purple and blue. The grand robe was woven from the best Trimber material. He stood behind the seat of Armbruster and awaited the arrival of the commanding pair. He held the Ceptre of Argin. The sphere, a dark blue color, with its middle swirling in a circular motion; the center gave off a white, intense light. The Ceptre signified power and it was greatly respected by others.

Armbruster had given Yarlen the Ceptre with its magical 'seeing sphere' as part of his change of power ceremony. It signified

Yarlen's position as Head Seeier, the only one to see changes in the sphere. The Ceptre was believed to allow Yarlen to view into the future or see special events, both good and bad.

Quiet chatter continued until Armbruster walked through the door holding Queen Alexis' arm. He guided her toward the throne and assisted her as she sat down. She smiled at him and looked straight ahead at the rest of the council. Armbruster sat next to her and folded his hands. He tucked his feet beneath his Warlock Command robe. Everyone sat quietly. Yarlen quietly stepped away and sat in the front row, facing the Queen and her Warlock husband.

Within seconds, the door opened. The Narry was the first thing everyone saw, followed by Carmin. Everyone turned their heads to watch the arrival of the baby. Carmin walked into the Hall wearing her lavender robe. Her long, black hair pulled back into a very large bun. She smiled as she guided the Narry toward the stage. Once there, she snapped the Narry into the silver throne in front of Alexis and Armbruster. She then stood behind the couple, remaining close but out of sight.

"Witches, Warlocks, council members and visitors….it is my great pleasure to announce the arrival of my beautiful daughter and your future Queen, Grand Princess Lilah of the Lunar Council. Please, be so kind as to remain quiet as we induct her into our council, and our great Alstromia," Armbruster announced.

He lifted the child out of the Narry and proudly displayed her for all to see. Ahhhhhh's and Oooohhh's could be heard throughout the Hall. Everyone was taken-back by the beauty of the child. The baby, now fully awake, looked attentively around the room and seemed to smile. Her eyes sparkled; her beauty seemed to hypnotize most.

Armbruster walked to the table by the window. There, the head of Council performed the Ritual of Newcome to welcome the child, and to officially give her the title of Grand Princess

Lilah of the Lunar Council. Once the short process was complete, Alexis kissed the child's forehead and asked Carmin to take her to Visitation Hall, where the celebration would take place.

"I want to thank you all for your attendance. It is my pleasure to have you witness this new and exciting event…the introduction of your new Princess. Thank you all for your kind wishes. We thank you, as well, for the lovely presents you have bestowed upon us."

Alexis sat down on her throne and changed her demeanor. "Now, I must address a few things. Surely, most of you are aware of the new Council and Order we have established. Some of you are less than pleased with the changes. Let me be clear – if you do not like it, too bad! This is how it will be from now on. If you have issues with this leadership and council, feel free to move back to Iriss. Perhaps you will like it better there? I am sure my sister, Zandorah, Head Witch of Solara Council, will be more than happy to have you in her clan. I am not interested in having anyone here on Alstromia that is not willing to comply with the new rules and regulations. This leadership is looking to make history. If you do not want to be part of it, leave. I know this sounds harsh…but it is reality."

She stood up, walked down the three steps, and approached the seated council members in the front row. She stopped in front of Aerianna, her best friend, and smiled. "I want you to become my Second in Command. I want nothing more than to have you sit next to me and Armbruster, as we plan the rest of the new changes. Please, accept this new position," she stood impatiently awaiting her response.

Aerianna smiled and rose quickly from her seat. She bowed to Alexis and placed her palm up, to receive the purple Gem of Elight. This gem was only given to those closest to Alexis, and receiving it was a huge honor. It would be worn in a special headpiece to signify Elite Council. Alexis placed the glittery gem into Aerianna's palm and cupped Aerianna's fingers around it. "So be it," she declared.

She smiled and turned, as she walked back to her throne. She sat down and announced: "please welcome Aerianna – Fanna of Alstromia…my Second in Command. She is to be respected and feared. She will be assigned her own personal security. I will expect you to treat her with the respect she deserves," Alexis watched as other council and visitors congratulated Aerianna, some with obvious jealousy.

There had been a rumor Aerianna would be elected by Alexis but no one knew for sure, mainly because many thought Armbruster, her husband, would be her Second in Command. However, Alexis felt Armbruster had too much responsibility as Head of Warlocks. She did not want to worry about his lack of attention toward her needs and plans. She had every intention of making Aerianna her Second in Command, because she knew Aerianna would do whatever she wanted her to. She had spent hours contemplating about how she would change the council, and who would perform what job, in this historic and new leadership. Armbruster continually whined about her vision and ideas. He reaffirmed her belief it was best to keep him out of her plans. It was a much easier plan this way.

Aerianna sat down in her chair and held her precious gem. She grinned at Alexis in delight, knowing they would make a powerful pair. She had a long history with Alexis. They had grown up together and had always been a powerful combination. She knew in time, Alexis would officially make her part of the Council. Aerianna was honored. She had dreamt of this moment, and replayed the scenes in her mind many times. At night, she contemplated how she would be able to help guide Alexis in her decision making. It was an exciting time filled with endless possibilities. She was elated. Aerianna knew she was not just a friend to Alexis, but also someone who would help Alexis realize her goals and vision for the future of Alstromia. She was more than willing to make sacrifices for her beloved friend, Alexis.

"Everyone, please be seated for one more moment. I have a final announcement to make. I would like to thank you all for your attendance. I invite you to join us for a welcome banquet for Princess Lilah in Visitation Hall. We will also hold the Change of Title for Aerianna there at the same time," Armbruster announced.

"Yes, please leave the Hall," chimed in Alexis, always wanting to have the last word. She looked at Armbruster with disgust. Why did he always have to speak? He greatly irritated her at times, and this was one of those times. She looked away, frustrated with Armbruster.

As the council and visitors left the Hall to make their way to the reception and food festivities, as well as the Change of Title affair, the room became very quiet. Alexis stood up and walked to the window. There, she surveyed the scenery below. She felt good, knowing she was in control. Alexis was convinced more than ever she'd made the right choice in Aerianna. Armbruster tapped her arm and informed her it was time to join the others. She harshly pushed his arm away. "Go. Go ahead. I will stay here for a little while, as I have a headache. I need some time to myself," irritated, she rolled her eyes. She blatantly ignored him, staring at the valley below.

Armbruster shook his head and instructed Carmin to take the child back to her chamber and change her clothes. He planned to meet his Warlock Command Team for a quick conference before attending the royal festivities.

Carmin left to tend to Lilah.

chapter 2

Enforcing Power

Alexis sat on a stool by the window. She daydreamed of her future and the powerful, new kingdom. She was very hopeful. As she gazed out the window, she looked at the valley wondering if all she had planned would go smoothly. As she took in the scenery, she realized how much she disliked the view. The moment she had arrived on Alstromia, she felt the valley was much too cheery and bright. She simply did not care for it. The whole atmosphere needed a makeover! She had every intention of bringing the environment up to her standards and to make it the gloomy, dreadful place she wanted it to be.

She reluctantly agreed to erect her palace at the highest point, Grandu Peak, overlooking the valley. Alexis adamantly disliked the bright light and glorious scenery. She was not impressed, missing the dark valley on Earth, where she previously resided. She loved the dark, musky castle in New England, America, and missed the rain. As she thought about the details of Earth, she realized one of the things she missed most was the rumble and shaking of the powerful thunder, and especially the bright flashes of lightning. She sighed, as she reminisced about fighting with humans and playing wicked tricks on them. There was so much she missed.

Looking at her current scenery, she felt frustrated and sad. Somehow, she convinced herself she could start a new life here and make it a better place for all witches, without human interference. She did not miss being harassed by the humans or being hunted down like a wild animal. Humans were worthless creatures; she was glad she no longer needed to deal with them.

The night she fled Earth, she vowed never to return. She knew it was the best decision, at the time. Armbruster, however, kept expressing his dislike for their abrupt departure from Earth. He wanted to remain in contact with their friends and planned to visit them back on Earth. Alexis adamantly disagreed with Armbruster. Somewhere or somehow, in her heart, she knew those humans would eventually turn on them as well. Humans could never be trusted. She had learned this unfortunate lesson too many times on Earth. Armbruster believed in humans and admired their character. He wanted to believe they could be trusted. Alexis felt Armbruster was very naïve. She despised his weakness and thought his trust in humans was misplaced.

Life on Alstromia was far better. It contained zero humans and she was in total control. She would decide how it was run, and who or what could visit or remain on her planet. It was about control. She felt as if for the first time in her life, she had gained complete control. Now, all she had to do was get Armbruster to see it her way, or dispose of him as well. She preferred not to get rid of him, as part of her still cared for him very much. She was torn by what she wanted and by what she knew she needed to do. It was never easy being the Queen of Witches.

Her gaze caught Torrins flying up to the landing deck below, pulling the carriages, delivering Witches and Warlocks to this monumental event. She spotted a few familiar faces. Aerianna was below on the deck, welcoming VIP's to the event, mostly from other Councils.

Aerianna was in her full glory. She looked stunning in her dark, purple cloak. Her long, curly, blonde hair, which always looked somewhat unruly. However, the look seemed to work for her. She was a rather tall woman with long legs. Her face was breathtaking. She had full, bright-pink lips. Her eyes, large and a deep chestnut color. Her most stunning feature were her amazing, long and fluttery eyelashes. Aerianna was also very blessed with a tiny waist and voluptuous body. Alexis had always been very jealous of Aerianna's gorgeous figure and features. However, she would never admit it to anyone.

Off in the distance, the twin moons glistened in the darkening evening sky, giving off an eerie glow, while casting a soft light on the valley. The wind was soft and warm. It was a wonderful evening, which would be filled with fun, excitement, and most of all, unexpected events!

In another room, further down the long corridor, Armbruster talked with his Command Team about changes he had planned. He insisted on increased security, as some of the other Councils would surely want to sabotage the new Order about to take place on Alstromia. Armbruster was also highly concerned about the safety of Lilah and Alexis. He instructed the Guard of Command to be on high alert and ordered the team to circle the Palace on their Torrins, securing the perimeter. Armbruster did not want any interruptions while they celebrated and held the festivities. It was his responsibility to keep his wife and child safe. He worried more than most, and never seemed to be able to relax. Ever since leaving Earth, he felt a bit more relaxed, but still believed other Councils (and clans) wanted to sabotage all they were trying to establish on Alstromia. In his heart, he knew in time things would be great on Alstromia.

However, he still deeply missed Earth and his human friendships. He wished Alexis would understand his need for human interaction and friendships. She scolded him about the humans and repeatedly demanded he cease all communications with them every chance she had. It irritated him. Often, he thought about returning to Earth. However, now he had a child. He also still loved Alexis, though she had changed – not for the better. He sighed and looked off into the distance, as he thought about his time on Earth.

Alexis stepped away from the window and walked to her chamber. She changed robes, opting for her Grand Ceremony gown. It flowed to the ground with a purple, pearlescent glow. She picked up her silver, crystal-encrusted brush and brushed her lustrous, black, hip-length hair. She looked at herself in the mirror and smiled. She was ecstatic all the visitors were about to witness part one of her new plan of change, it made her tingle with delight. Alexis knew Armbruster would not approve, but she really did not care. Too bad. Her eyes twinkled and she felt a rush come over her. She was ready. She was about to make the change of a lifetime.

She walked to her closet and withdrew her tall, Star Ceptre. The hand of the Ceptre had a lizard-like texture. Affixed to the top was a blood red square-encrusted gem, surrounded by tiny stars. When Alexis cast a spell or transported herself, she would slam down her Ceptre, causing the silver, sparkling stars to produce an opaque fog.

She raised it to the ceiling and shouted: "in the name of Sonia, give me the power!" Instantaneously, she felt a small jolt vibrate through her from head to toe. She laughed and shook her head in glee as she walked toward the door. There, she stopped. She looked at herself in the floor length mirror with self-adoration. Alexis liked what she saw - beauty and power. What a great combination, she thought. She knew she was about to make history. Alexis had never been shy about expressing her vanity or denying how proud she was of her own accomplishments. She considered herself a visionary, believing she was set to become the greatest Witch ever! She walked out the room, feeling confident, ready to start a new beginning. She slammed the chamber door shut and rushed down the corridor.

Armbruster sat at the head table in Visitation Hall. He looked to the right side of the table, and observed Yarlen speaking with

Garlow, his son. Off to the left, he saw Aerianna looking smug, with her new Gem of Elight in her Elite Council Head Circlet. He did not like Aerianna, as he knew she was obsessed with power. She was always looking to make changes he felt were radical. When Alexis unfolded her plans to bring Aerianna into the Elite Council, he became quite annoyed. He had been very vocal, letting her know it was a huge mistake. He realized it was irrelevant, Alexis would not listen. She had made up her mind, insistent on not changing it. She was simply informing him of her decision, not asking for his approval. Alexis never asked, she did what she wanted, when she wanted. At one point, it was something he admired about her, but now, it was the one thing he truly disliked. Having Aerianna as her Second in Command would only signal future problems. He did not like it.

Aerianna knew what Alexis had planned for the celebration, but was also keenly aware Armbruster would be furious. She did not care. She would support Alexis and her vison for change. Aerianna tapped her long fingernails on the side of the table as she waited for Alexis to arrive. She looked around the room and admired the large crowd filling the room. What a great turn out, she thought. Aerianna was happy for Alexis and Lilah. Armbruster, however, was another story. She did not get along with Armbruster and had long ago realized it was better to stay out of his way. She kept her relationship close to Alexis and made sure she remained civil to Armbruster, only to please Alexis. Aerianna knew, having Armbruster as an enemy would not be a good thing. He still had many powerful connections and it was best not to mess with him. Aerianna was not stupid, after all.

The Hall filled with laughter and talk. The crowd seemed happy, boisterous, and very unaware of what was about to happen. Numerous local Council members mingled with Council from other planets, including Earth. Many were busy looking for assigned seats around the big tables strategically placed throughout the room.

Warlocks and Witches were separated and seated in order of command, by district, or clan. Other visitors sat in the back, along the end of the room. Their view was not the best, but they could see the event, nonetheless.

Security guards could be seen in every corner of the room. They held Mesmer Ceptres, prepared to protect the Palace, if necessary. They wore black, mid-length robes, with their trousers tucked into boots. Looking out the windows, you could see Security Guard of Command patrolling on their flying Torrins, vigilantly circling the castle. Security was at its highest level for this event, so ordered by Armbruster himself.

Alexis entered the Hall. Everyone immediately stopped talking and quickly took their seats. She walked confidently to her seat, next to Armbruster, and looked directly at Aerianna. Alexis smiled and Aerianna reciprocated. Armbruster touched her hand gently, nodding in approval, only to have it swiped away. "Not now," Alexis hissed with a frown and total impatience. Just you wait, she thought.

Carmin walked into the Hall with Lilah in her Narry. No one spoke, they only watched quietly. Carmin placed the Narry behind Alexis and was dismissed. She walked to a stool and sat down keeping an eye on Lilah.

Armbruster stood up clapping his hands. "Witches and Warlocks, may I please have your attention? I would like to thank you again, for your attendance. We will be starting our celebration with food and drinks, followed by the official Change of Title for Aerianna. Please, have fun and enjoy this monumental event. This truly is an evening of celebration!" He sat down quickly, not wanting to extend it longer than necessary.

Suddenly, somewhere deep in his mind, he tried to dismiss the feeling as if something horrible was about to happen. He wanted this evening to be perfect. Something was not right, he just knew it. He started to shake and feel nauseous. His right eye twitched. He rubbed it briefly, feeling concern. Beads of sweat pooled over his bushy eyebrows. His face felt flush as he heard his heartbeat in his ear thumping.

Everyone applauded his announcement. The large doors swung open and the wait staff entered, pushing large carts overflowing with plates of food and drinks. Good smells permeated the room. The staff walked around, filling up tables to feed the hungry crowd. Other staff members filled the oversized glasses on the tables with famous potions and drinks. Everyone in the room seemed to be having a great time. It was a lively event and a true celebration.

Alexis looked around the room and scooted close to Armbruster, cupping her hands over his ear and whispered: "Enjoy this my love, it is what we have waited for." She scooted back into her seat and smugly winked at Aerianna. She ran her right hand through her hair, pushing some stray strands behind her ear. At times, she wished she had shorter hair. It was so annoying to have it fall over her eyes, blocking her view. Maybe she should cut it all off? No, probably not. She was just irritated. No need to do anything radical with her looks for now, she thought.

Armbruster looked at Alexis perplexed. What did she mean by her comment? Was she sincere or was it a mixed message? The bad feeling in his stomach grew. He muttered: "excuse me dear, I will be right back," as he proceeded to stand up and walk toward his security team.

"I have a bad feeling in my stomach. Please, have everyone on the lookout. I do not know what we are looking for, but something feels off. I do not want anything to ruin this evening, have I made myself clear?" The head of the Security Council nodded his head, signifying he understood the responsibility. He swiftly walked off to talk with the rest of his team, barking out orders.

Armbruster turned and walked to the double door, wanting to

check on the outside security team as well. However, as he tried to open the door, he found it was locked! Stunned, he spun around to see Alexis stand up. Instantly, his heart skipped a beat, making him feel dizzy. He knew something was very wrong. He stood in shock and disbelief, waiting to find out why she was standing, looking ever so self-righteous. He knew she was going to do something awful.

"Everyone, may I please have your attention? Armbruster, sit!" Alexis ordered. She motioned for him to sit down, pointing to his chair with her long, bony finger. "I would like to inform everyone that I have ordered all doors locked. The windows have been sealed and no one is leaving until I am done talking." Instantly, everyone panicked and looked around nervously. Most did remain quiet though, generally because they were scared and unsure of what was happening or what was about to happen.

"Aerianna, please come sit by me." She gestured to her friend and confidant. "I have made the decision to let you all know my secret plan. Those of you here may or may not be part of it. However, you will not be leaving the Hall, until you have a complete understanding of what I am about to do. You are invited to decide where you want to be, and if you want to be part of this new plan."

Feeling weak, confused, and upset, Armbruster grabbed the closest chair and sat down. He was shaking and violently pissed off. His gut feeling had obviously been correct. Somewhere in his mind, he had known something was wrong. He hated the fact he was correct. He listened to Alexis, watching a woman he no longer knew. He was greatly disappointed, Alexis was out of control. He gazed over at Aerianna in disgust, knowing she had been up to no good, plotting this moment with Alexis.

Aerianna had accepted an invitation by Alexis to move into the palace to be near her side. Armbruster had tried to convince himself she was there simply to help Alexis during the difficult pregnancy. Now, he knew there was more to that story. He felt ill. Bile filled his mouth and it made him feel horrible. He grabbed a glass filled with Porting Wine off a nearby table and guzzled it. He felt woozy. What was happening? The security team stood by and did nothing. He knew right then and there, she had arranged something with them. They were under her control and he had lost his power!

"As many of you know, I am sickened over the bright and sweet environment of Alstromia. We moved here to Alstromia to start fresh. I do not want our new home to be so damn fluffy and happy. The current condition does not reflect the true environment I envision for Alstromia. We are Witches and Warlocks, for goodness sake! We are powerful and should be feared. We should not be subjected to this unsatisfactory, happy, and cute atmosphere. With that said, I will be casting a spell to immediately change the planet, to reflect a more appropriate environment."

She raised her Star Ceptre and exclaimed: "Let the light reflect the mood, for now I see what is good." Suddenly, everything outside became black. Lightning flashed, adding an eerie glow to the dark, night sky, as loud, pounding rain poured out of dark clouds. Alexis squealed with delight. Aerianna smiled and clapped with joy, much like a small child. Others looked stunned, simply mumbling under their breath. Armbruster lowered his head and tried to keep himself from crying. He rubbed his pounding temples. He could not believe what was happening. Armbruster shook his head in disbelief and closed his eyes. Everything was swirling around him.

"Finally, a proper atmosphere for our new adventure. I ask for your patience while the surroundings change. If you are not happy with the change, please consider moving to the planet Iriss, with my sister Zandorah, Head Witch of the Solara Council. She is a much kinder, gentler, and softer witch. Perhaps, those of you who are weak, would prefer to live under her power? If so, please step forward so we may transport you to Iriss as soon as possible. I do not want anyone weak in my clan or council. So, rest assured you may leave."

Armbruster stood up. "Alexis, I beg you to reconsider. May we please speak privately?"

"I will speak with you later, Armbruster. You are not well; you may be dismissed. Yarlen, take Armbruster to his chamber," she ordered. The large double doors unlocked and Yarlen stood up as he walked toward Armbruster to guide him to his personal chamber. As they exited, the doors closed with a bang and relocked.

"Anyone else feel like they want to leave?" Alexis inquired. There was silence. A small witch in the back raised her hand. "Grand Queen Alexis, I would like to be excused. I would like to take my family to Iriss."

"So be it, take your leave and never return. If I see you in my clan, or near this planet again, you will be destroyed. Do you understand?" hissed Alexis.

"Yes, very clearly. Thank you." The young woman approached the doors. They popped open, allowing her to leave swiftly. The doors closed again, but this time did not lock.

"I invite all weaklings to leave immediately. This new Order is only for the strong and visionaries. You should not stay if you do not want any part of it."

Several witches and warlocks walked to the door and left the Hall. After a few moments, no one else left. Everyone else present remained seated, quietly. Alexis stood up.

"Good, I see my loyal followers have stayed. Let me say, thank you. You will not be sorry you stayed. Let the new changes begin now." The light dimmed in the room. On the right wall, next to the head table, the massive fireplace ignited with bright, purple and green flames.

"Now, let's have some fun!" shrieked Alexis.

Alexis turned to Carmin and asked her to take Lilah to her room. "Please, watch over her and make sure you take a security officer with you."

"Yes, I will do so now," stated Carmin. She unsnapped the

Narry and guided it out of the room toward Lilah's private chamber. Once there, she instructed Pauto, a security officer, to stay and keep guard. He smiled and reassured her all would be okay.

On the other end of town, near the river of Miccay, the three met in secrecy. They sat huddled around a small table in a dimly lit room. The commoner's cottage was the perfect, inconspicuous place to discuss their strategy.

"The plan is perfect! You morons better know your part. My future depends on it," bellowed the tall and muscular figure. He sat across the table, staring at the other two, squinting his eyes.

"Sir, it is brilliant. We know exactly what must be done," replied Bartin, squirming in his seat.

"If you mess this up, you will be sorry. I cannot, and will not, allow you two to destroy all we have worked for...you better be prepared!" He slammed his fists down on the table, causing it to shake. Bartin apprehensively looked at his acquaintance, hoping he would say something. However, he remained silent, scared of any repercussions. He knew it was best not to say a word.

"If all goes well, I shall regain my power, and she will pay..."

Carmin dressed Lilah in her sleeping gown. Once done, she placed the baby in the fluffy crib. She gently covered the sleepy child. Carmin proceeded to walk to her own bed on the other side of the large room. She plopped down on the top blanket and closed her eyes. She could not believe what had just happened. She admired Alexis, but now feared her. She wished Armbruster had done something to stop her, but realized he no longer had any form of control. Armbruster had grown weak, Alexis had won.

The noise of the rain hitting the window lulled Carmin to sleep. She heard echoes of thunder in the distance, reminding her of nights on Earth. She smiled, as she drifted off into a deep sleep. She never heard the baby's soft cry, as a tall, dark figure lifted Lilah from her crib.

chapter 3

Kidnapped!

"Help! Help! OH NO…the Princess has been kidnapped!!" screamed Carmin. She ran down the hallway looking for Pauto, or any other security member, almost tripping over her own feet. As she turned the corner of the corridor, she bumped into Armbruster, almost causing him to hit the wall.

"What are you saying?" he screamed, as he violently grabbed Carmin's arm. "Where is my child?" his eyes flashing in anger.

"Sir, last night I put the Princess in her crib. I woke up this morning to feed her and she was gone. I went to the Queen's Chamber thinking she might have Lilah, but she does not. Sir, she is gone; she has been kidnapped!" Carmin fell to the ground shaking and crying, her head buried in her hands, tears running down her cheek.

Armbruster shook his head as he looked down at Carmin. Stupid woman! Why had she not protected his daughter? Angry, he turned and ran down the hall. Just as he was about to turn another corner, he encountered a security commoner with a Mesmer Ceptre in his right hand. It appeared the security commoner was already aware of the missing child and had initiated a massive security sweep, scouring the Palace looking for the missing baby. Security was on its highest alert. Still, Armbruster did not like the fact she had not already been found. This, most likely, meant she was not in the Palace – Lilah had in fact she had been kidnapped. He became violently angry. He quickly pushed aside the security commoner and turned to find Alexis. She was undoubtedly in her chamber. He never made it to her chamber, as he spotted her approaching with pure anger on her face.

Alexis came running down the hall and grabbed Armbruster by the arm. "What have you done?" she screamed at him. "My child is missing because you are weak. Find my child or pay the price." She released his arm and took a swing at him. He stopped her hand an inch before his face.

"Stop it, Alexis. You are out of control! I understand you're scared…but enough! Gain control of your emotions, others are watching us," his eyes wide-open with anger, his bottom lip sticking out.

Frustrated and disgusted with Armbruster, she turned and ran off to find Aerianna. Armbruster was deathly afraid. He had no idea who had taken his child. The audacity, he thought. He wondered if it was someone close to him. Was it payback for Alexis and her new plan for the clan? He felt ill all over again. If this was retaliation because of Alexis' grand new plan, she would pay and he would personally see to it. Her irresponsible actions could have prompted the kidnapping.

Aerianna shook her head in disbelief as Alexis told her about Lilah's disappearance. She was stunned and could not believe what she heard. Alexis seemed uncomfortably calm, considering her child was missing. It made Aerianna wonder how she was able to remain so cool.

"What are we going to do, Alexis? Who do you think took her? Why did they take her?"

"I am not even going to try to guess. I will tell you one thing for sure, whoever took her will be sorry and they better hope she comes home unharmed, or they will surely perish!"

Aerianna watched as Alexis paced back and forth. She was

clearly becoming more agitated as time progressed. Her demeanor changing rapidly.

Down the hall, in another chamber, Armbruster sat in a circle with four other Warlocks planning their next move. Orin, his trusted friend, explained how he had heard someone walking outside earlier in the morning and ordered security to check it out. Unfortunately, nothing unusual had been found. Suddenly, the door blew open, and a breathless security member entered, struggling to speak. "Calm down, my friend. Take a moment," Armbruster advised.

"Sir, two of the Torrins and a carriage are missing. It is the Queen's carriage. It is gone! What are your orders, Sir?" he stood at attention, waiting to hear Armbruster's response.

"Go back to the rest of the security. Tell them to take the rest of the Torrins and conduct a security sweep. They must find the carriage. I want it found immediately. Do you understand?"

The security commoner bowed his head in acknowledgement and left swiftly. He had a mission and was not going to fail. He proceeded to walk down the steep stair case to find the other security members to give them the new orders. Within minutes, seventeen young commoners mounted Torrins, and flew off into the morning to find the missing carriage and Princess.

Meanwhile, Alexis sat by her window crying. She rubbed her eyes. It had been a long time since she felt this out of control and she did not like it. Alexis was grieving the disappearance of her daughter. Why had this happened? She seethed. It better had nothing to do with Armbruster, she thought. However, her gut feeling told her it had everything to do with him. Perhaps it was related to his growing incompetence as a leader. Time would tell. Armbruster had become a liability and she knew she could no longer rely on him. Alexis would take things in her own hands. She would enlist Aerianna's help, she was more than capable.

Alexis realized the front of her gown was soaked with tears.

She got up from her chair and walked toward her closet to change out of her wet gown. There, she took out one of her favorite robes, a dark gray, flowing robe with purple crystals embedded in the sleeves and neck. She loved the feel of the material, it soothed her when she was upset. Once she was wearing the gown, she returned to her large and plush chair. She placed her head in her hands and sat quietly. Suddenly, the door flew open. Armbruster entered with two guards.

"I have news! We found one of the drivers of your carriage. He was knocked unconscious. He saw the face of the thief and claims it was a woman. She wore a purple robe with silver Darbeds. You know, the only ones wearing Darbeds are the witches from Earth!"

Immediately, Alexis stood up and walked toward Armbruster. "What are you saying, Armbruster? Was it my mother? Was it Lorthana? Answer me," she screamed, hysterically.

She pointed her finger right in his face and continued her tirade, "If it was Lorthana, I will tell you this……she will perish by my hand. Mark my words." Clenching her fists, she pounded the air, grinding her teeth. Her eyes flashed like lightning from anger, as she stared at Armbruster with a vicious scowl.

She stormed off to her royal Meeting Chamber, two guards on her heels. Her black hair flowing behind her, like a long, black veil. She was furious. How dare that woman, she thought. Why would Lorthana do this? Did she really think she would get away with kidnapping her child? Her mother was insane. Alexis would ensure the traitor paid with their life.

Opening the large, double doors to the royal Meeting Chamber, Alexis frowned.

"Get Aerianna in here now!" she shrieked at Pershiah, her personal assistant. Pershiah looked at her for a moment, with confusion on her face. "Lazy girl, did you not hear me? Get off your big behind and go get her now." Scared to death, Pershiah ran from the chamber to find Aerianna. Alexis watched her quick departure, smiling and feeling amused.

At the same time, Armbruster appeared in the royal Meeting Chamber with his guards. He tightly held the book of Varathune in his shaking hands. He looked deep in thought, as he mindlessly tapped his finger on the book, staring at Alexis.

"Alexis, we must read the Detector, and possibly enact the Chant of Reztec. We must ensure safety for the clan and kingdom. Please! I know you are upset. However, we need to protect all of us. If Lorthana took Lilah, then she will be okay. She will not harm our child. She is merely trying to send you a message. Plus, we do not even know for sure if she is the one responsible."

"You must think I am an idiot. Of course, it was Lorthana! My mother told me when we left Earth, she would make me pay for betraying our family and leaving. This is her way of sending me a very clear message." Alexis stood up from her chair and walked toward Armbruster. "Why do you insist on being so protective of her? Hmmm? What is it you know about this?" She glared at him as she shook her head in disgust. He squirmed uncomfortably in his stance, still tapping the book.

"Exactly what are you accusing me of, Alexis?" he growled back, with his head cocked off to one side. He knew exactly what she was implying and it angered him. Why would she think he was protecting anyone? Why did she doubt his loyalty? He had not given her any reason to feel this way.

"Oh, let's not play games, Armbruster. You know exactly what I am saying to you." She rolled her shoulders and glared at him. She felt betrayed. She stood in front of him with her hand on her hips. Alexis believed Armbruster was withholding information.

The chamber opened and Aerianna entered. Her eyes red, swollen, and puffy. She looked awful. She was wearing her red robe, indicating mourning. This only seemed to aggravate Alexis more as she watched Aerianna enter the room.

"Finally, what took you so long?" she hissed, looking at Aerianna. She looked at the red robe and shook her head with contempt. "How dare you wear the Robe of Tears? Remove it at once. I cannot believe you would do that. She is not dead, she is simply missing!"

"My Queen…I simply wanted to honor your feelings of loss and grief during this difficult time. Please, accept my apology! Of course, I will change at once."

"No. Hold on, Aerianna," interceded Armbruster. "You are right, we should all be wearing our red robes. We need to show the commoners and those around us that this is a difficult time. We must show unity. We should all change our robes!" added Armbruster. Aerianna was shocked. Had he just agreed with her decision to wear the robe? Wow, that was something new. She bowed down in front of him and looked down. He placed his hand approvingly on her right shoulder. "Go sit, and let's talk," he demanded.

"Okay, enough already. We will all wear our robes, happy, Armbruster? Can we please get on with it already?" replied a snippy Alexis. She could not understand why all the irrelevant chit chat. Why the debate? This was a waste of time.

"The driver stated it was a woman with astonishing green eyes," relayed Armbruster. He continued, "also, he stated he saw some of her hair from under her hood. He claimed it was jet black. She was also very tall. I can only assume it was Lorthana, based on the description. There is no one else we know matching that description other than her. So, the question remains, what do we do? Shall we go back to Earth to find Lilah? Shall we send a Hunt party to find Lorthana? How do you wish to proceed, dear?" he asked Alexis looking straight at her. She looked away and walked to the window. She had heard enough. Alexis was convinced it was Lorthana. She bit her bottom lip, not wanting to yell. Silence filled the room. She took a deep breath to regain her composure. She would tell them exactly what she wanted them to do.

"I want you to do whatever you have to do to find that woman. I want her delivered to me in one piece. I want to be the one to put an end to her miserable life. It will be my hands that will drain her life. I want the honor. If she kidnapped my child, she will DIE!"

Armbruster bowed his head and walked out the chamber. He was certain what had to be done. He had no problem with delivering Lorthana to Alexis. If Lorthana was responsible, she would have to pay the price. Alexis would not stand for this betrayal. For once, he agreed with her.

Lorthana walked down the narrow corridor of her estate. She carried the Book of Bartue in her left hand. She was in a hurry to find Gardone, her husband, and speak with him about Alexis and Armbruster. Lorthana knew Gardone would want to figure out where to look next for the pair. She entered his room.

"Hello, dear," she whispered, trying not to disturb him but still get his attention.

"Oh, hello! Come in Hana," replied Gardone. He always called her Hana, especially when he was in a good mood. "What may I do for you? Is that the Book of Bartue? Are you still trying to find them?" he asked, knowing the answer, wondering why Lorthana had not yet given up.

"Gardone, you know I want to find them. I can only assume they are on Alstromia. However, the Globe of Sight is not showing me anything. I have not found them. Zandorah has not heard from them in a long time. She is very worried and annoyed as well."

"Well, maybe they want to be left alone, they were in a hurry to leave. You should respect their wishes. I know you miss her, Hana, but you must let it go. It is just hurting you more every day. She will come to her senses one day and return, I promise."

"You know, dear…the thing I love about you most, is the fact you are such an optimist. However, I know my daughter. She is headstrong and very stubborn. Well, kind of like her mother. She will not come back here, ever! It breaks my heart as I think of her daily. I cannot even enjoy being a proper witch here on Earth, knowing my daughter is not here to share all the fun festivities," stated Lorthana.

"Time will heal all of this, trust me. I must go now, to attend the weekly meeting. I will be home later. Go relax and enjoy the full moon." Gardone walked out of the room and into the dark hall with his attendant, Cheeve, right behind him. "Come on, don't walk so slowly. We are late," Gardone reprimanded Cheeve.

On the way out the door, he stopped by the tall shelf to pick up his Ceptre of Stainnard. It had been given to him by his father, the Great Warlock Prince Stainnard. It was a powerful Ceptre. The power was not known to most, as it was a secret weapon. However, Gardone knew its power. He was well aware of how it worked and used it in his favor to solve issues. With the Ceptre of Stainnard, he was able to locate Alexis and Armbruster the moment they arrived on Alstromia. He knew exactly where they were, and did not really care. They were traitors, and like all traitors, they would pay for their abandonment. He walked to the Wizzor Hall, where the meeting was taking place, to decide how to deal with the traitors!

Back on Alstromia, Alexis sat in her chamber for hours, looking out the window feeling hopeless and powerless. She desperately wanted her daughter back in her arms. She missed her smile and the cute, pink lips. She adored her gorgeous, sparkling eyes. Frustrated, she rose from her chair and marched toward the door. She was about to grab the handle, when the door popped open, almost hitting her in the face.

"I beg your pardon…. what are you doing? Are you trying to kill me, dumb girl?" she shouted at Carmin.

"Excuse me, your Royal Highness. I am so sorry. I was just going to ask you if there was anything, I could do for you?" she bowed meekly before the Queen, keeping her head low, showing respect.

"No, there is nothing you can do, unless you know where to find my child?"

"No, I am sorry, I do not. I wish I did. May I be excused?" stuttered Carmin.

"By all means, leave!" she dismissed her, waving her hands. At times, she really disliked Carmin. What a worthless, little witch. She acted more and more like a commoner...no common sense what so ever!

Carmin left the chamber and ran to her room crying. She felt horrible, and the Queen continued to make her feel guilty. She had nothing to do with the disappearance. She would give her life if it meant getting the Princess back. She loved Lilah the moment she had met her. She felt responsible for her and the kidnapping felt personal. She had failed the Princess. Once in her room, Carmin drew the curtains closed and crawled under her blanket. There, in complete darkness and silence, she cried herself to sleep.

Alexis walked quickly down the hallway. A few of the workers bowed before her as she passed them. She did not acknowledge them, just simply kept walking. She was not in the mood to deal with them. Commoners, she thought!

Armbruster gathered his men in his chamber to talk. They discussed the urgent need for tighter security. One of the warlocks suggested the Chant of Reztec, a chant to secure the entire planet. Armbruster had already talked with Alexis about performing this Chant. It would require ten different warlocks to make it work and none of them could be from the same clan. They would need to be different Guiders. Armbruster liked the idea.

"How many different Guiders do we have on Alstromia? Does anyone know?" asked Armbruster, looking at the group of warlocks.

"Sir, I believe we have up to twenty-five. However, only eight are in our direct line of command. I suggest we interview all twenty-five to see which Guiders can help us perform the Chant of Reztec. It would be the best plan. Do you think the Queen would help? Her Ceptre is powerful enough to be equal to two or more Guiders. What do you think?" questioned Harshim.

"No, Harshim. I do not want to involve the Queen, she is mourning. She is not herself. I need you to focus on bringing the twenty-five Guiders to me today. Are you up to the task?"

"Of course, Sir. I will go with Samoine. He will help me. It will take two or more hours…. I mean mims, but we should be back before the evening. I am sorry, I forget the Queen does not want us to use Earthly terminology. I apologize. Also, I promise not to take long, as I realize we must expedite this process. Hopefully, we can get it done before the morning."

Harshim walked out of the meeting and yelled, as he demanded for his assistant Samoine to join him. They jumped on two Torrins, pulled back on the reigns, and flew off to Miccay to find the twenty-five Guiders. At the same time, the others sat in silence and observed Armbruster, wondering what he was planning. He sat with his right hand against his cheek, tapping on his face. He looked deep in thought. Suddenly, he turned toward the others. His eyes grew big, his eyebrows raised.

"I have an idea. Let's go to the Carriage stable and speak with Essten and ask him where his son is hiding. He was not at the stable this morning, I find this very peculiar. I think we need to make it clear we need to speak with him. Perhaps he saw something or knows something," announced Armbruster feeling empowered.

The others nodded their heads in agreement. They thought it was odd Collan was not around. He was always tending to the Torrins, braiding their manes and brushing them. He had been their keeper for years. It seemed suspicious he was missing.

Minutes later, Armbruster walked up to Essten, looking at him with a scowl. Essten had been expecting someone to show up to ask about Collan, but he never thought it would be Armbruster. He bowed down and stammered "Your Royal Majesty…how may I be of assistance? Are you wishing to fly one of the Torrins? I can retrieve your favorite one," he smiled, hoping it would hide his nervousness. A small bead of sweat ran down the left side of his face. He quickly wiped it away.

"We are not here to fly, we are here for Collan! Where is he? He was not here when my security came by and they claim he is missing. So, where exactly is your son, Essten?" Armbruster asked with a tone of interrogation.

"Sir, I have not seen Collan in a while. He did not come to the stable to feed the Torrins today. I came by to bring food and he was not here. My wife informed me he has not been home either. I have no idea where he is. Please, accept my apology for his absence. I promise the moment he arrives, I will send him your way," announced Essten, nervously. He really did not know where Collan was hiding and he was getting worried. No one had seen him since the day before. It was not like Collan to be gone for long. He loved taking care of the Torrins and took his job seriously.

"Well, that will not do. No, not at all. I want him found now!" He pointed to the house behind the stable. "Search the hut; search the grounds. Find him. I want him found. Is that clear?" he barked at the security detail behind him. They nodded in agreement and walked off to start the search.

"Sir, he is not here. I am not lying to you. I have been loyal to you and your family my whole life. I promise! He is missing."

"Essten, I believe you do not know where he is hiding, but we will find him. Let me tell you, if I find out he had anything to do with the disappearance of my daughter, he will die! Do you understand? I hope you comprehend what I am saying," he raised his Ceptre and pointed it at Essten, as it projected a beam of light. Immediately, Essten felt nauseous. He bent over and began vomiting. He looked up and wiped his mouth. "Yes, I understand." His entire body felt rubbery. His stomach ached and his head felt like it was about to explode. He swallowed and tried to keep from vomiting again.

"Good, now go get cleaned up. You look and smell disgusting," Armbruster shouted at Essten.

Armbruster lowered his Ceptre. He hated having to do that, but he wanted this commoner to be sure to understand what he was capable of doing to him. That was just a tiny, painful, message to make him hurt and to make it clear he meant business.

Armbruster felt alive for the first time, in a long time. He felt in total control. Everything was about to change. He was not going to back down until his daughter was found. The one responsible for the kidnapping would pay. He would watch them suffer at the hands of his wife, Alexis, and would enjoy watching her destroy the kidnapper.

"Sir, we found this by the back of the hut," security guard Porti handed Armbruster a black cloak, embroidered in Darbeds. It was saturated with blood and also torn in two areas. Armbruster frowned as he realized, it was a woman's cloak. The robe was also very long, definitely belonging to someone tall. He shook his head. He accepted the cloak from Porti and flung it over his right shoulder and declared "I am off to see the Queen. Keep looking. Anything else you find, give to Yarlen. He will ensure I get whatever it is. I want Collan found, is that understood," asked Armbruster. He was not happy. He was keenly aware Alexis would not like this new information. He had to find a way to break it to her, slowly.

Armbruster walked back to the Palace to find Alexis. He was convinced, more than ever, Lorthana had something to do with the audacious kidnapping and feared for her safety. If Alexis felt her mother was responsible, she would ensure Lorthana would be held accountable for her actions and suffer greatly. He disliked the idea of telling Alexis about his suspicions. Worse, he hated thinking about showing her the cloak. He took it off his shoulder and rolled it into a ball and carried it behind his back. It would be better if she did not see it right away. He would have to find a way to bring it up, and then show it to her. Most likely, there would be little he could do to prepare for the moment. However, he would try to find a way to sneak it into the conversation.

Armbruster entered the Palace and ran into Aerianna in one of the hallways. He asked her if she had any idea where he might find Alexis. She pointed to the balcony, off to the right side of the Hall of Visitation. He thanked Aerianna and proceeded to walk up to Alexis, holding the cloak behind his back. Alexis looked at him sideways, with an odd look on her face.

"What are you hiding from me, Armbruster?" she inquired.

"Now, what makes you think I am hiding anything from you?" he smiled nervously, baring his teeth. He knew what she meant, but was not ready to share the news or show her the cloak.

"I suppose, I know you too well. I also see your arm is behind your back. Now, why would that be? So, fess up. What is it?" She was getting annoyed at the game he was playing with her. She knew he had something he wanted to show her. She could only assume it had something to do with the kidnapping or Lorthana.

"Sit down, Alexis. I need to talk with you."

"No, tell me now! I tire of this game…what is it?"

"Here." He pulled his hand out from behind his back and showed her the bunched-up cloak. Before he could say anything, she noticed the Darbeds. She could feel the anger rise quickly in her body. She became stiff, as she stared at the cloak in disbelief.

"Is that my mother's cloak? Where did you find it? Where is she?" She touched the cloak. "Is that blood? What is that?" She shook her head. So many emotions all at once. They hit her hard. She rubbed her stomach. She cupped her hands over her mouth and looked at Armbruster, feeling ill.

"Yes, it looks like it. It feels and looks like blood. No, I have no idea where she is. No, I do not know if it is her cloak. My security found it by the stable. I had gone to ask Collan a few questions. Unfortunately, he is nowhere to be found. Essten reported he has been gone for a while."

"Really, and you believed that?" She rolled her eyes at Armbruster, skeptically.

"Oh yes…he is telling the truth. I used my Ceptre. He does not know where Collan is, trust me."

"So, what about Marittaz? Does his mother know anything?" She suspected someone was protecting Collan. It probably was Marittaz.

"We could not find her either, she was not home. My security is looking for her as well," added Armbruster, seeing the reaction on Alexis' face. Alexis was not good at disguising her feelings. When she was mad, it was apparent. She looked beyond mad.

"Marvelous! All the ones we need to speak with are missing. Do you not find this odd? My child is gone, and no one has a clue where she is! I am telling you, someone knows something." Her tone escalated in range indicating her patience was dwindling quickly.

"Yes, Alexis, someone does know something. We just need to find the one that knows the correct information. We will find him or her soon enough. I have something I am working on. I am trying a few things," Armbruster announced feeling very sure of himself.

"Trying? Really? Well, that does not make me feel confident in your abilities. Trying is for losers. I need results. Perhaps, I should take over this task?" Alexis pointed her Ceptre at him in anger. "You completely amaze me with your 'trying' comment. I am stunned you would even say that."

"Don't you dare threaten me. Do you understand? You may be Queen, but I am still your husband and leader. Don't you ever forget, without me, you would not be Queen. DO YOU GET IT?" he screamed right back at her in anger, his veins bulging out of the sides of his head; his bushy eyebrows arched high, and his voice louder than it had been in years.

Alexis backed down. She had not heard him that vocal in a long time. She saw pure rage in his dark eyes. At that moment, she feared him. She looked away. Hmmm, perhaps there was still hope for Armbruster, she thought.

"Yes, I understand." She took the cloak from his hand and left the area. She headed to her chamber. In the hallway, Aerianna took the cloak from her hands and walked behind Alexis in silence.

Armbruster paced back and forth, trying to calm down. He had not been that angry or nasty with Alexis in a while. He was frustrated and outraged with her, mostly appalled at her attitude. It was time. He would remind her and the rest of Alstromia he was still the one in charge. She was a Queen, a figure head, but he was the one maintaining control. Things needed to revert back to the way they used to be. She needed to be controlled and he would be the one to do it.

He walked back to his chamber. He placed his Ceptre on the shelf and sat in the chair by his desk. He remained silent. Just as he was about to open a book to read, he heard a loud knock on his door.

"Come in," he shouted in an irritated tone.

"Sir, I bring exciting news! I just came back from talking with two of the commoners and they had some news to share."

"Okay, spit it out! What is it?" asked Armbruster very impatiently.

"Sir, one of the commoners who was responsible for taking the Torrins back to the building after the arrival of special guests noticed something unusual. He noticed one of the Torrins was not yellow, it was the rare, white kind. It was also not friendly, it kept trying to fly off. The commoner had to tie the beast up in the dark stable, to keep it from getting out. Its owner must have come privately to retrieve it because when he came back later to check on it, it was gone!"

"Really? Well, that is interesting." Armbruster was even more convinced that Lorthana had a part in the kidnapping. His wife's mother was the only owner he personally knew with a white Torrin.

He smiled. Finally, a clue worth investigating. He would keep this information private for now until he had more news. He was not going to tell Alexis until he was convinced Lorthana had been the one involved in the kidnapping. Alexis would jump to conclusions and potentially ruin the investigation. She had to be kept out of it for now. He smiled.

"Thank you. You are dismissed. See Yarlen and you will be rewarded."

"Oh, thank you kindly, Sir! I appreciate it." The commoner walked out of his room.

chapter 4
Revelations and Betrayal

Lorthana placed her favorite cloak on the end of her bed. It was filthy and required washing. She would have Stellah clean it when she was done cleaning the rest of the Estate. She wondered what the status was with the hunt for her daughter. She missed Alexis. She also worried her husband knew something he was not willing to tell her. However, she knew better than to question him. Last time she did, he nearly destroyed her. He was not always very loving, and at times, harsh and violent. He lacked patience. He did adore his daughter, but there was something evil in his heart. She made a point of staying out of his way most of the time.

She looked out the window and saw smoke billowing out of a chimney from a house down the river. She wondered if the humans knew she lived in the Estate on the mountain. Lorthana walked to her messy desk and sat down. She looked through a pile of pictures and smiled. Her daughter's picture lay on top. She picked it up and admired her beauty. "Where are you, my beautiful child? Why did you leave me?" she asked as she started to sob. She wiped away her tears. She sat stoic, looking lovingly at the pictures.

The door to her room opened suddenly and Zandorah appeared.
"Hello, Mother!" she said.
"My goodness. What are you doing here? When did you get here?" Lorthana she walked toward her daughter and embraced

her. Zandorah swiftly pushed her aside. "Enough of the warm hugs and smiles. Mom, I need to talk with you about something quite serious."

"Well, what is it?" inquired Lorthana, looking at her daughter.

"Are we alone? Is Dad around?" Zandorah looked around the room nervously. Lorthana could tell something was wrong.

"No, your father is at the weekly meeting, why do you ask?" She was starting to feel a bit uneasy about the line of questioning. "What are you up to, Zandorah?"

"Mom, Lilah is missing. I know who did it."

"What? What are you saying? Alexis had the girl? They named her Lilah? Why is she missing? What is happening?" asked a confused Lorthana.

"Mom, calm down. Yes, Alexis had a girl – Princess Lilah. They held a ceremony and performed the Ritual of Newcome. That night, Lilah was taken from the Palace on Alstromia, where Alexis and Armbruster reside."

"Okay….and how do you know all this? I don't know any of this," screeched Lorthana.

"Mom, Dad has known for a while. He told Shawnatar and Shawnatar told me. I have no idea why Dad is keeping it a secret. Do you think he had something to do with the disappearance of Lilah?" as she said it, she wanted to retract it. She feared her father. He is very powerful and most clan members fear him. She had left Earth with Shawnatar for that reason, fearing for her own safety. Shawnatar was both her husband and her dad's good friend from the Clan of Tarbo. They had known each other for a while. Though Shawnatar was much younger, they had been good friends and grown powerful together in their magic. Shawnatar and Gardone still communicated and kept each other's secrets. Well, for the most part. Shawnatar did not hide things from Zandorah and believed his wife deserved the truth. So, he had told her the Earthly minute he found out where Alexis was with Armbruster.

"Why would your father hide this from me? He knows how worried I have been about her absence," asked an obviously perturbed Lorthana.

"Ask him yourself, I have no idea. He is always hiding things, you know this! I am here to share some things with you. For one, Alexis and Armbruster are on Alstromia…as I stated previously. Two, Lilah is their new child. Three, Lilah has been taken. Four, I know who took her and I fear when they find out, they will kill me. Mom, what should I do?" Zandorah quivered as she spoke, almost stuttering. It was apparent she was very scared. She looked pale. She seemed restless and unable to stay in one spot, walking around while she talked with Lorthana.

"Okay, hold on. How do you know this? Who did this evil thing? Tell me and I will protect you!"

Zandorah started to laugh hysterically. "What makes you believe for one second you can protect me? You have NO idea who we are dealing with. Even Dad cannot protect me. Trust me. We are all doomed!" She threw herself in the chair and began to cry. Her long, brown hair falling around her face. Lorthana walked over to her daughter and bent down. She looked up at Zandorah and moved her hair away from her face. "Zandorah, look at me. It will be okay. Tell me everything you know. Do not leave out anything. I have to know every miniscule detail. I want to help."

Zandorah looked deeply into her mother's eyes. She wanted to tell her, but she feared the worst. She looked away, shaking her head repeatedly. Zandorah knew this was a horrible situation. She hated the fact she knew so much. It put her life in danger and those around her as well. Her mother would want to help, but ultimately, her life would be in danger too.

"Mom, it was Loggane! He dressed as a woman and kidnapped the Princess. He did it to get back at Alexis. He used your cloak. He stole Pica, your Torrin! Oh no… We are all dooommmeed."

She began to cry, sobbing loudly, shaking and rocking back in forth with her arms wrapped around her belly.

Lorthana stood up and shook her head in confusion. She looked down at Zandorah. "Get yourself together, child, we must meet with the Clan immediately. Get your cloak and let's go!"

Lorthana grabbed her green robe from the stand by the desk and threw it on quickly. She zipped it up and made her way to her bookshelf. There, she grasped the Staff of Itma. The moment her right hand touched it, the glow became a radiant, bright green. She smiled at Zandorah and raised it up high. Both witches stood side by side. Lorthana slammed the Staff of Itma to the ground, chanting. Green sparks disbursed through the air. The two were enveloped in a green haze and disappeared.

On Alstromia, Armbruster paced up and down the hallway by his chamber. He shuffled his feet, dragging his long cape behind. He twirled his Ceptre around in a circle, unaware of the ominous, red light emanating from it. Eventually, the light became very bright. He had to put the Ceptre away to contain its magic. He smiled, as he thought about using it to destroy the one that had taken his child. Quickly, his smile faded though. He remembered Alexis making it clear she would be the one to destroy the kidnapper. So be it, he thought. Let her do it. He would watch with great delight, enjoying the impending torture.

His mood was glum. Aggravated, he walked toward Alexis's chamber. He knew they needed to talk. She had been ignoring him, spending all her time with Aerianna. The two were most likely plotting something. She had taken the Book of Aches into her chamber and ordered Aerianna to research spells to impose the most hurt, to the one she would destroy. Obviously, she was blinded by her hatred and anger. She had lost focus. She was not thinking about the child. Rather, her entire mission was set to destroy and hurt the one responsible for her child's disappearance. How absurd. Why not focus on finding the child first? Armbruster became frustrated. Alexis was out of control and Aerianna only fed into the frenzy!

He knocked on her chamber door and walked right in without waiting for a reply. He opened the door to find Aerianna sitting next to Alexis looking at the book. They both looked up at the same time as he entered, with an irritated look.

"Can I help you with something?" Alexis hissed at him.

"My, my, my. What a great way to greet your loving husband," he sarcastically replied.

"What is it you want, Armbruster?" added Aerianna with a self-satisfied look on her face.

"I am here to speak with my wife. You may leave, Aerianna."

"She most certainly will NOT leave! Stay, Aerianna. Whatever he has to say to me, you can hear," snarled Alexis. She rose from the chair and walked toward Armbruster.

"What do you want? I have a lot to do and you are wasting my time. Speak already...." Once standing in front of him, Alexis gave him a look of disgust. She intently stared into his eyes, hoping to make him feel uncomfortable.

"Aerianna get OUT!" he shouted. He raised his Ceptre toward her. She felt uneasy and ran toward the door. "I will be back," she yelled as she closed the door. Aerianna knew it was best to exit quickly, she did not want to experience Armbruster's wrath.

"Do you feel better now? Why did you have to do that? You are so rude." Infuriated, Alexis glared at Armbruster. She despised his lack of control and quick temper.

"Silence! I have something to tell you. Not everything we talk about concerns your best friend. Now, shut your mouth and listen for once," he demanded. He shook his head, looking Alexis straight in the face. She had a way of bringing out the worst in him. He hated it because it made him feel less in control. Alexis was a great manipulator. She knew how to push his buttons and obviously enjoyed watching his reactions.

Alexis walked to the fireplace and sat in the large chair. She squinted her eyes, glaring at him with anger. "Fine, say what you must," she sarcastically responded, knowing she had upset him.

"Alexis, my security team has received word that Zandorah knows we are on Alstromia. Also, your father called a weekly meeting to discuss our disappearance from Earth. I know this because I have spies on Earth to help protect us. Zandorah supposedly also knows who took Lilah. She is meeting with Lorthana as we speak. I think we should bring Zandorah here. She is not safe on Earth!"

"So… my sister knows who did this? Why are you not on Earth retrieving and questioning her? For all we know, she had something to do with it," retorted Alexis.

"I do not believe she had anything to do with the kidnapping. She claims to know who did it. Her life is in danger. Shawnatar is in danger. If you do not care for Zandorah, I know you care what happens to Shawnatar," he murmured, looking directly at her. He knew without a doubt that statement would make her change her mind. He believed Alexis still had feelings for Shawnatar after all this time. If anything, she would request Shawnatar be brought to Alstromia. She would not allow the love of her life to be in danger. Now, Zandorah was a different story. Alexis would have mixed feelings about her sister's safety. Their relationship had been ruined over Shawnatar, neither wanting to fix or discuss the situation. They were both very stubborn.

Alexis looked away. Instead, she focused on looking directly into the flames of the fire. Sitting next to the fireplace she felt warm, but shivered. Thinking about Shawnatar brought back all sorts of memories and emotions. The one she had loved more than life itself, only to be taken from her by Zandorah. She would never forgive her sister for the betrayal! Yes, Armbruster was correct. She cared for Shawnatar and would want him here. She wanted him safe, even if Zandorah wasn't. It did not matter to her what happened to Zandorah. She had betrayed her and their sisterly love was no more.

"Send out a Hunt team to retrieve them from Earth. I want them here and I want answers," she growled. Armbruster approached Alexis to console her, but she merely brushed him away. "Go on, get it done! Do what you do best. Leave!"

He shook his head in defeat and walked to the door. He turned around to watch her stand by the window. He knew Shawnatar was on her mind, her one true love. He had always known there was no way he could compete. He had stopped trying a long time ago. Now, he had to deal with his presence once again. Armbruster despised the idea. However, he knew it was out of his control. Alexis had ordered his presence. So be it.

Armbruster walked out the door, proceeding in the direction of his chamber. Halfway there, he saw Aerianna speaking to one of the older Clan Witches, Tamarah. He stopped to say hello, hoping to hear what they were discussing. Tamarah smiled sweetly and excused herself as soon as she saw Armbruster approach. Aerianna looked at Armbruster, her head tilted to the side.

"What? Is there something else I can do for you?" She looked at him with repugnance.

"Yes, as a matter of fact there is. You can go take care of my wife, she is not well. Protect her and be there for her. Act like her friend. For once, stop thinking about yourself." Armbruster walked off without saying another word. He had made his point. She irritated him so much. He wished she had not come to live in the Palace. Aerianna was becoming too much like Alexis, and that was not a good thing.

Aerianna watched him walk down the hall and wondered what was going on. She was going to find out. She would ask Alexis the instant she saw her. Armbruster was becoming too vocal and much too snippy for her liking.

Aerianna entered Alexis' chamber in a huff. She was perturbed about her quick, one-sided conversation with Armbruster. As she walked up to Alexis, she could tell she had been crying a lot. Her eyes were swollen and red. Her face was wet from tears. She looked dreadful. Her was hair messy and sticking to her cheek.

"What may I do for you my friend?" she asked Alexis as she observed her.

"Did you know, Zandorah and Shawnatar are aware we are here? Did you know, they are on their way to Alstromia? Armbruster is getting a Hunt team together to bring them to me. Supposedly, Zandorah knows who took my precious little girl. He will have no choice but to tell me. Trust me, I am not going to allow her to lie to me. I will not tolerate her lies or complete disregard for my feelings." Alexis threw her cup at the wall and watched it shatter into pieces. She was furious. How dare Zandorah keep secrets from her, she thought.

Aerianna walked to the broken glass, bent down, and proceeded to clean it up. "Don't touch it. I will have someone else take care of it. I do not want you performing menial jobs." Alexis yelled for Karita, one of the commoners. She entered the chamber quickly, cleaning up the broken glass as ordered, and hastily left the room.

Alexis and Aerianna sat in silence. Loud thunder boomed outside, causing the massive window to rattle. The only other noise to be heard was the crackling of the fire in the fireplace. Finally, after a few moments of complete silence, Aerianna spoke up.

"What do you want to do, Alexis? Do you have a plan? Is there anything I can do for you right now? I know you are bitterly upset!"

"No, there is nothing you can do. We must wait to see if Armbruster can retrieve them from Earth. I can tell you with certainty, I am getting more impatient. It has been almost a day since my precious child has been taken from me. None of the spells are revealing where she is. This is so odd. Someone must have cast a Concealment Spell. Even Armbruster stated it is unusual, and he usually knows all. He instructed Yarlen to use his Ceptre as Head

Seeier to find her.... yet nothing. I am beyond anxious." She walked to her bed and threw herself on top, her feet dangling off the edge. She laid on her back staring up at the ceiling. She did not know if she wanted to scream or cry. She folded her arms and continued to look up, not saying a word. Nothing made sense to her, the situation was out of control. Alexis did not like the feeling, it evoked too much anger.

Armbruster burst through the door with Yarlen. Alexis sat up quickly and looked at him puzzled. "What is it?" she asked quickly.

"They found Shawnatar but not Zandorah. Your mother, Lorthana, is gone too. No one knows where they are. Your father is at home waiting for their return. He promised he would let me know when they return. I think we should be prepared for anything at this point. I am afraid there is something awful going on and it directly involves Lorthana and Zandorah. Unfortunately, I have no idea what. Yarlen, did you see anything?" Armbruster looked at his Second in Command, hoping he had good news to share.

"No, Your Majesty. My Ceptre is not showing me anything. It is as if the Princess simply vanished. She is nowhere to be seen." He shook his head in disbelief and anger. Yarlen did not like telling Alexis and Armbruster he lacked the ability to 'see' the child. After all, it was his responsibility and job, as Head Seeier, to be able to see everything and provide valuable information. Something was wrong. His powers were not working. No matter what he did, no matter what he tried, there was nothing to be seen. Yarlen felt useless and it made him frustrated. He did not want the Queen or Armbruster blaming him for his lack of ability to find the child.

"I was just explaining to Aerianna, I believe there is a Concealment Spell over all of this. Otherwise, we would be able to see something," added Alexis. She looked proud, as if she was adding something of value to their conversation.

"I agree. However, you know as well as the rest of us, reversing the spell is virtually impossible. Yarlen, where do we stand with the Chant of Reztec? Did we find the required Guiders to perform the Chant?" questioned Armbruster, observing his friend. Yarlen was quick to respond.

"No, we found eight, but that is not enough. I will go speak to the rest of the Guiders and see what we can do. I shall return as quickly as I can. I am not sure why we have been unable to locate enough Guiders." He hastily left the chambers and headed to the Hall. He knew he would need to figure out something. Armbruster and Alexis were losing their patience with the entire process, it was taking too long. Alexis was not a patient witch and she would not allow this to go on forever. She liked structure and planning. Nothing so far had been planned well. Likely, she would eventually take things in her own hands. Alexis would involve Aerianna because she was just like her, power hungry and driven. The situation would only get worse, and not better. Yarlen knew it was up to him and Armbruster to find a way to diffuse the situation and find the child.

"What do you want to do, Alexis? I have done what I can. I think I am going to retire and sleep, I am beyond exhausted. You should do the same. Do you want me to stay and keep you company?" Armbruster asked Alexis, knowing the answer in advance. She would not allow him to stay.

"No, I want to be alone. I am going to sit here and figure it all out. I have a lot to consider. Thank you, though." Alexis knew he had tried. Unfortunately, he had failed. Armbruster always failed her when she needed him the most. She had stopped relying on him a long time ago. She simply pretended to ask for his assistance, to keep him believing she still trusted him, even though she did not. Alexis knew he was not capable of being the warlock he had once been. He had lost credibility among the clan and turned soft. She wished he would regain his stamina and become the warlock she had fallen in love with – strong, powerful, and relentless.

Armbruster looked at Aerianna and gave her a dirty look,

disgusted with her. He wished she was back on Earth. She was always there, right next to his wife. He was never allowed to be near Alexis anymore. It was an outrage. He stormed out the room and slammed the door. Enraged, he changed his mind about sleeping. It would be better to join Yarlen and the rest of the Guiders in the Hall of Visitation.

Aerianna shook her head, angry with Armbruster. Why did he have to be so mean all the time? The nerve of him. He was making everything more difficult for Alexis. Did he not understand Alexis was already upset? She did not deserve Armbruster's lack of self-control. Aerianna took the book off the desk and tucked it under her arm. She turned around as she stood by the chamber door.

"Alexis, I hope you get some rest. I will look through the book for some spells. There must be something we can do. I will meet with Farla to see if she has any suggestions. After all, she is the one with the most knowledge of spells. I promise, we will find something." She gave her a pretend smile and walked out of the room, leaving Alexis to think. Aerianna held the book close to her body as she walked down the dark corridor. Her heart raced as she thought about Farla. She was feared by many because she was so powerful. However, Aerianna realized they needed her help. Farla was possibly the only one capable to counteract the Spell of Concealment. She was very gifted. Most thought she was a bit eccentric. She was short, stout, rather mouthy, and not the kindest of witches. However, she was more capable than most. Thus, many kept their opinions about Farla to themselves.

Armbruster entered the Hall of Visitation and sat down with numerous Guiders. Several of them had great advice, but none knew what to do. Yarlen looked pale. His usual flushed cheeks looked ashen. His hair was not tidy, nor pulled back into its ponytail. Rather, it looked wild and messy. He was not doing well. Perhaps, he felt guilt over not being able to see anything of value to help Armbruster or Alexis. As Head Seeier, he should have been able to help. Maybe, he felt as if he had failed them? It possibly was a huge weight of guilt on his shoulders. Yarlen slumped in his chair, reflecting his negative mood.

"Guiders, please be quiet. We must pull together. We currently have eight Guiders to help perform the Chant. This is good news, we only need two more. I believe there are two other Guilders in the next village over. One of you will need to go there tonight to find them. Arlow and Camrun are very capable Guilders and we could use their assistance. They will be ready to go if we ask. The Chant must be performed by the end of the night. So, hurry. Bring them back immediately," ordered Armbruster.

"Yes, Your Majesty. I will take a Torrin and go now," replied Hamptin.

"Excellent. You are a true friend, and most valuable Guider. Thank you. Be safe!" responded Armbruster. He was happy to see Hamptin stand up. At times, he was a bit on the shy side and not too forceful, though he was a very talented Guider.

The rest of the Guiders remained in the room planning the event of the night. The Chant of Reztec was very complicated, requiring certain items to make the Chant work. All magical items were held in the Tower, a storage facility in the palace. Only those authorized could enter this high-security area, but Armbruster elected himself to retrieve the items.

"Yarlen, will you assist me in retrieving the necessary items? I could use your help," requested Armbruster. He handed Yarlen a huge black bag from the table, a magical Chant Bag. The bag was deep and able to hold heavy items. It was constructed of material from the inside of Trimbers, known for its durability and hardiness. This part of Trimbers was often used to make bags or boxes, and could also be woven for additional strength. Yarlen took the Chant Bag and flung it over his shoulder. The two Warlocks left the Hall and walked toward the Tower, which was at the other end of the Palace. Outside the room, however, Yarlen stopped.

"Sir, there is something I have to tell you. You are not going to be happy about what I have to share with you. I apologize in advance. I'm sorry," Yarlen confessed in a high pitched and squeaky voice.

"Well, what is it? Tell me. You know I trust you."

"My son, Garlow, saw one of them. The evil ones, the ones who took the Princess. He was too scared to tell you. He was worried you would think he had something to do with it. He went to Earth to find them."

"What are you saying? Are you telling me he knows who did this?"

"He believes it was Loggane. Your sister's son - your nephew. I did not want to say anything, until we knew for sure. I am sorry I kept it from you. I just wanted to be sure. Now, I believe you need to know no matter what." Nervously, Yarlen walked on, hoping Armbruster would take the news well.

"You did the right thing by telling me. I am not mad. I am a bit taken back by the fact you did not tell me before. Do not worry about it, I trust you. I know you are always an ally. Your intentions are well known and I trust you with the well-being of my family. Honestly, if I did not trust you, you would not be here." Armbruster put his hand on Yarlen's shoulder. He was not mad, simply annoyed by the whole situation. The two continued their walk toward the Tower. Neither spoke.

Meanwhile, Alexis put on her long sleeping gown and brushed her hair. She took a swig of her drinking potion and placed the glass on the table next to her bed. She called Karita to tend to the fire. She could have used magic, but it was more enjoyable to make Karita work. She was a bit lazy and Alexis felt the girl needed to work for her keep. Karita, a tiny commoner, had come to work for her a long time ago. She had come highly recommended by Essten.

When Alexis first met Karita, she acted so nervous, accidently spilling a drink on Alexis. Karita assumed she would not get the job. However, Alexis surprised her by giving her the job anyway. Alexis thought the girl had handled herself well, despite her clumsiness. Karita was also not very intelligent, which Alexis thought was a bonus. It would not be difficult to keep her out of her business.

Once the fire roared, Alexis crawled into her bed and drew the covers up to her chin. She watched the fire from her bed and thought about Lilah. Tears started to flow from her big, green eyes and ran down her cheek. She started to sob, her heart aching. All she wanted was to have Lilah back in her arms safe and sound. How could she go on without her? Would she ever see her little Princess again? Her head was hurting so much. Alexis closed her eyes trying desperately to think about other things. Slowly, she drifted off to sleep, still slightly sobbing.

On Earth, Lorthana and Zandorah popped into the Chant Chamber in the Hall of Wizdom, known to be the most powerful place for Witches on Earth. The cylinder-shaped building was constructed of aging, irregular shaped blocks. It covered in moss and ivy, blending inconspicuously into the woodsy scenery. Inside the building, the entry was large and bare. A massive stone stairway led to the basement and the Chant Chamber.

Lorthana put her Ceptre behind her back and walked toward the Chant Circle, to join the others. One by one, each Witch placed their Staff or Ceptre outside the circle. They sat on the gigantic, red pillows on the painted, peeling concrete floor.

"Clan Witches, I need your help. As some of you know, my daughter, Alexis, left Earth with her husband Armbruster. She recently had a child, Princess Lilah. On the night of her welcoming and the Ritual of Newcome, she was kidnapped! Zandorah, my other daughter, is here with me today. We are seeking your assistance to keep the forces away that try to destroy us. We need your immediate help. Please, let me explain further," announced Lorthana, looking attentively at the group.

Lorthana spent quite some time explaining the entire

circumstance to the Clan Witches. After she was done, the room became very quiet. Clan members looked around nervously, not sure how to respond. No one wanted to be the first one to speak.

"What exactly do you need from us, Lorthana? I understand you need protection, but what are we to do?" asked Chynah, a red-haired Clan Witch. She smiled, but looked perplexed.

"Yes, we can help cast spells, however, they will not work unless it is for those on Earth. I am confused. What specifically are you asking us to do?" chimed in Starlitte. She was a tiny and young Clan Witch with great protection spell abilities. It was her greatest strength.

"I am asking for any assistance to keep Zandorah safe. As I stated, she is in danger. Until we find the one that kidnapped my granddaughter, Zandorah is in danger. I would hope, we could unite and become a powerful force against this evil. I humbly ask you to join me in any way you can." Lorthana stood up and walked to the oval table by the fireplace. She placed her Ceptre sideways, facing the clan. "I am at a loss. You know I am not a mean witch, but I am more than willing to be aggressive if need be. My daughter's life depends on it. I have not yet met my grandchild. Can you imagine? Some of you know how protective I am of those I love. I will fight until the end to protect my family. Can I count on you?" she boldly asked, looking directly at the group.

She waited for a response. Suddenly, everyone stood up. They walked toward Lorthana and Zandorah. They encircled them. Zandorah and Lorthana stood in silence, while the rest of the Clan Witches chanted their protections spells. Once complete they smiled, feeling relieved. It was a moment of reassurance. They were safe, though possibly just for a while. Hopefully, the chant had worked well enough.

Not far away, a small group of Warlocks met in a dark room. One of the Warlocks wore a green cape, with only his eyes visible. He smiled under his cape knowing soon he would have what he wanted. There was no doubt, Alexis would pay for her betrayal. He was tired of waiting; the time had come. He glanced down at the tiny child in the wooden crate. She looked beautiful, and he could not help but see Alexis in her. Yes, she was definitely the mother of this child. She would never see this child again, as long as he was in control!

He walked to the next room to meet with the other Warlocks to discuss the next step in their plan. It was a brilliant and well thought out plan to take back power. He was about to regain his power, it was just a matter of time. Now that he had what Alexis wanted more than anything, he knew she would negotiate. He had no doubt. His smile widened as he thought about his impending victory.

chapter 5
New Beginnings

Shawnatar sat quietly at the table looking through a variety of old, dusty books. He could not believe Zandorah had just left like that with no notice of any kind. What was she thinking? He thought about Armbruster and the fact he probably told Alexis everything they had hidden from her. She was most likely aggravated by now. He missed watching her eyes widen right before she would laugh or scream. He missed her pouty smile. Well, he just missed her, though had learned to live without her. He told himself he loved Zandorah. It was easier this way, for everyone. Yes, he was being a good friend to all… or so he wanted to make himself believe.

He shoved one of the books off the table and onto the floor. He was miserable. He had tried for years to forget about Alexis. Now, she had a child, though not his. It was Armbruster's child…his best friend. It was difficult to accept. Suddenly, he felt enormous guilt. Was it his fault the baby had been kidnapped? Was it someone he knew? Was it someone that knew he still loved Alexis? Did any of it have to do with him, or perhaps Zandorah? He had so many questions.

Still angry, he walked to the fireplace and threw a book into the flames. He watched it catch fire and burn. He wondered why it made him feel better. He laughed out loud, alone, in the room. He snatched his Chant Robe from a chair, and headed to the next room to meet with the other Warlocks. He wanted to ensure all was being done to protect Alexis and Zandorah. He wanted Lilah found as well. These were difficult circumstances. Somehow, he knew things were going to work out. However, he feared someone else would might be hurt before all was done. He was terrified at the thought it could be Zandorah. He pushed the thought out of his head as he opened the door to the Meeting Room. It took only a second. The pain hurt so great. He closed his eyes as he fell onto the hard, concrete floor.

As his eyes fluttered about to close, he looked up briefly and saw him! Loggane was smiling down at him with a wicked smile. His statuesque and muscular body was towering over him, looking smug. His bold, blue eyes danced with delight, watching Shawnatar pass out. It was the last thing Shawnatar remembered before becoming unconscious.

"Someone put him on the large couch over there," Loggane pointed to the large, brown couch by the wall. "Hurry up. I want him tied up. I do not want him to get away," ordered Loggane.

"Sir, I am not sure he is still alive, he is bleeding a lot. What should we do? Shall we fix him manually or perform a spell?" asked Markis, as he watched the blood running off Shawnatar's head dripping onto the floor.

"Check on him and keep him alive. I need him. Do whatever it takes."

Loggane walked over to take a look down at Shawnatar sprawled on the couch. He looked okay. What was Markis worried about? A little blood never hurt anyone. He was a Warlock. It wasn't like he would die so easily. He was still breathing. Loggane could not help but smile as he looked at the vulnerable being, passed out, not able to do a thing to defend himself.

"I am off to find the book in the attic. Get him cleaned up and put him in a new robe, he looks nasty. I despise the sight of blood. Clean it up," growled Loggane. He stormed out of the room and headed to the attic. He wanted to spend some time searching the library for the book. He knew there was a slim chance he would find it. Nonetheless, he was going to try.

Not too long ago, he had discovered the missing Spell of Concealment in an ancient book. Everyone believed the book had been destroyed. It had been his most precious discovery to date. He was quite proud of himself and wanted to search the library for other potentially powerful spells. Little did anyone know, he had many spells in the attic and would use them as he needed. A huge grin covered his face, thinking about what things he could unleash upon others with the spells he had waiting to be used. Spell power was a great gift and he planned to use it, a lot.

Loggane entered the makeshift library in the attic. The attic room was cold and dark. There were no windows or other exits, just one rusty, metal door. The area was well organized. It contained an extensive number of books. Some were very old, brittle, and falling apart. The shelves, made of wood, bowed from the heavy weight of the books. The room was also neglected and dirty, coated with dust and full of spider webs. Gigantic piles of papers filled an entire wall, stacked from floor to ceiling. Loggane had not attempted to scour through them to see what they were. He assumed they were someone's notes - worthless information.

He walked from bookshelf to bookshelf, searching for the right book. Where was the black book with silver print? He remembered seeing it a while back. He was sure it was here, somewhere. It could not just have disappeared.

Perplexed, he walked to the boxes in the corner and rummaged through those. He had tried previously to use his magic to locate the book, but was unsuccessful. It was bizarre. None of the spells seemed to work. Why was his magic not working? Was someone blocking his abilities? He was livid.

Loggane continued to frantically search through boxes and shelves. Nothing. Where was the book? Just as he was about to give up, he came across an interesting book. It was bright red, with bold, gold embossed letters. The book read: Enchantment. A simple title, he thought. He sat down on a nearby stool and flipped open the large book. As he was looking through the various chapters, he realized the pages were still in excellent condition. One of the chapters caught his attention – Concealment! He flipped to Chapter 9. He ran his crooked, long finger down the page until he found the word: Suppression. Instantly, he grinned from ear to ear. Victory!

Shawnatar tried to open his eyes. His head pounded. There was a screeching noise in his ears making him violently nauseous. He forced himself to open his eyes, one by one. Slowly, he opened them, attempting to squint, just enough to see. He spotted a fireplace, though it was blurry. He could faintly hear voices, possibly in another room. He struggled to move, but felt tied down. Frustrated, he looked ahead, trying to survey his surroundings. It became clear to him, he was still in the same building as before. He wondered, what had happened? Had he seen Loggane? What was going on? Shawnatar tried again to sit up. With much effort, he eventually managed to do so. Instantly, his head pounded louder than before. Boom…Boom…Boom…pounding, aching loudly. His head hurt. He licked his lips and tasted blood. He swallowed hard, trying to stay focused, though it was difficult.

Quickly, he realized he was tied up and could not move. He could not stand up without falling. He sat quietly and strained to think. It was proving very difficult with such a massive headache. Suddenly, things started to become clearer. He recalled putting on his cloak, walking into a room, only to be hit over the head. It was Loggane's face he remembered the most…smiling down at him, in an almost evil way. What had happened? Just as he was about to yell for help, he heard two voices getting louder as if they were approaching. He decided to lie back down and pretend to be knocked out. He slowed his breathing and closed his eyes.

"Seems like prince charming is still sleeping," noted Adoren.

He smiled, as he looked down at Shawnatar. "What a fool. I am so glad Loggane is taking care of all the weaklings."

"Yes, we certainly do not need anyone in our clan that cannot, or does not want to help Loggane regain power. Worthless...," growled Bartin as he looked at Shawnatar's body. Bartin touched Shawnatar's forehead. "He is getting a bit hot. Do you think he is okay? Loggane does not want him dead. What should we do?"

"Leave him. He will be fine. We must retrieve the potion from the Witch; it should be ready. We do not want to upset Loggane, again. This one is tied up, he is not going anywhere."

"Okay, if you think so. Let's head out."

The two warlocks left the chamber. The moment they were gone, Shawnatar sat up. Again, the familiar pounding in his head. His vision was still a bit blurry. He looked around to see if he could find any weapons. He saw a small object glistening on a nearby table by the fireplace. He dropped onto the floor and scooted toward it. There, he looked up at the table to see a small object, resembling a knife. He tried to grab it with his mouth. It took him four tries, but eventually he held it in his mouth. He dropped it onto the floor, while scooting closer.

Finally, he was able to grab it with his right hand. Quickly, he rubbed it back and forth, to cut the ties around his wrists. Success! He was free. He used the object to cut through the leg ties as well. Once he was completely untied, he stood up. His legs felt weak and shaky. He walked to the couch and sat down. What was he going to do? He put his hand on his head. Instantly, he felt warm wetness. He pulled his hand away from his head and saw dark, red blood. Nervously, he walked to a chair and grabbed a cloak. He placed it on his head, hoping to absorb the blood. After some time, it seemed as if the bleeding had stopped. He walked back to where he had been sitting and grabbed the ties. He threw them and the cloak into the fireplace. No need to leave evidence behind, he thought. He walked toward the large door. He propped his head up against it to listen. He heard nothing and felt it was safe to try to attempt an escape.

Cautiously, he opened the door. He peered around the corner to look for others. Nothing. There was no one to be seen or heard. He walked into the corridor, looking down both ways. Which way to go? He decided the best way was out. He walked as quickly as he could outside, though his legs felt like rubber. His head still felt rather queasy.

Upstairs in the attic, Loggane smiled. He knew what he had to do next. He also knew he would need more help to complete the next step. Obviously, he would take the lead, but he required the assistance of others. He disliked the idea of relying on others for help.

Loggane placed the book inside his cloak's large side pocket and walked down the stairs. He proceeded toward the great Chamber. Once he opened the door, he instantly noticed something wrong. Where was Shawnatar? Where were the idiots, Bartin and Adoren? They were supposed to be watching him. He became enraged. If they had taken him, they would DIE! If Shawnatar had gotten away, they would DIE…either way, they would DIE! His forehead scrunched in anger. He violently slammed down his Ceptre and disappeared.

Alexis looked at Aerianna waiting for a reply. "Well, what do you think?" she asked demanding an answer.

"Well, I think it does not matter what I think. What matters is that you are happy with the decision."

"I did not make you my Second in Command to have you act indecisive. Make up your mind and say so, I am not in the mood. You either give me your personal opinion, or there is no need for you to continue being my Second in Command," yelled Alexis, making her point.

"Alexis, I only meant…you need to do what you feel is appropriate. It is not up to me to tell you what to do."

"Listen, if I wanted someone weak and indecisive, I could have put Armbruster as my Second in Command. I put you in the position because you have always told me your opinion. Why change now? I must tell you, I do not like this side of you," Alexis walked to the fireplace and turned her back to Aerianna, her arms crossed in disgust, tapping her right foot.

"Very well then. I will tell you how I feel."

Alexis spun around quickly to look at Aerianna. She smiled at Alexis.

"I think it is a great plan. I think it will show everyone what you are capable of and that you are not going to accept anything other than their complete loyalty. I believe you need to act quickly though, Armbruster is trying to gain support. I believe he is trying to overthrow your power."

"WHAT? Are you sure?"

"I am very sure. Your loving husband suddenly wants to be in charge again, talking with Warlocks about changes. I think you need to be careful. He is going to betray you."

"Aerianna, be careful! You are accusing my husband of treason."

"Your Royal Highness, I am very well aware of what I am saying, and am also aware of the consequences of my words. However, I vowed to protect you and this planet. I have many spies. I was told Armbruster is doing many things, mostly aimed at regaining power."

"That under-handed, traitorous, back-stabbing liar. How dare he? I need immediate proof, Aerianna. We must put an abrupt stop to his actions. With everything going on right now, this is what he is worried about? Unbelievable. I tell you what, he will be sorry he did this. He will regret this until the last breath of his existence."

Alexis raised her Ceptre, closed her eyes, and slammed down the Ceptre as she chanted. She vanished. Aerianna looked around. For a moment she was upset, but then an evil grin surfaced on her face. It had worked. Everything would change now for sure. She would do anything to cause a rift between Alexis and Armbruster. She wanted to be next to Alexis when all was said and done, not Armbruster.

Armbruster listened attentively, as he heard a tale that made his stomach ache. So much betrayal, so many lies. Why? What for? He shook his head. Could he trust anyone? Yarlen looked at Armbruster and felt sorry for him. He could only imagine how Armbruster must feel. His own wife betraying him like that, horrible! He smiled nervously at Armbruster, who proceeded to stand up and pace back and forth, shaking his right fist.

"Are you sure?" he kept asking Porti.

"Yes, Sir! I am sure. I heard it with my own ears. She is planning to do it by tonight. Well, she was… before the child was taken. I am not sure if she still plans it for tonight or not, she might postpone it now. I do not know," Porti replied.

"I want you to get Aerianna. I want her brought here. Bring her alive. Do you understand, Porti?"

"Yes, Your Majesty. It shall be done." Porti ordered his guards to accompany him as he set out to retrieve Aerianna. He knew it would be a challenge. She would not come quietly nor willingly. She would use magic. They would need to be prepared and bring the Mesmer Ceptres.

"Sir, are you sure we can trust Porti?" asked Yarlen.

"Without a doubt. He has always been loyal. He would not lie."

"No offense, Sir, but many have betrayed you recently. How do we know who we can trust?"

"I casted a Respect Spell when he started sharing the details. It was the only way I could ensure he was being honest."

"Very clever! No wonder you are such a great leader. Always ahead of the game."

"No, not this time. I was totally unaware of her lies and deceit. I cannot believe she was going to have me removed. Who does she think she is? I have too many powerful friends and warlocks on my side, she does not stand a chance. She has lost her mind!"

"Perhaps it was the child birth? Do you think, it is what made her this way?" questioned Yarlen, looking for a reaction from Armbruster.

"No, she has always been this way. Now she is just power hungry. She believes that I stand in her way since I will not allow her to run me or do harmful things. That is why she wants me out of the way. I am sure she knows I would not go willingly. I am deeply saddened. My beautiful wife, a treasonous witch. I am going to put a stop to this, once and for all. I always felt this new leadership idea was an irrational one, I should not have agreed. I wanted to please her and make her happy. Look what I did, I created a monster." Armbruster looked defeated. He had tears in his eyes, looking devastated.

The loud pounding knock on the chamber door interrupted Armbruster's thoughts. "Come in," he shouted.

"Sir, we have found Collan," announced the security commoner.

"That is great news. Bring him to me, immediately!"

"Sir, he is dead!"

"What? Tell me what happened," commanded Armbruster.

"Sir, they found him in the River of Miccay. He …well, he is dead. Let's leave it at that."

"I want him. Bring him here to the Palace at once!"

"Yes, Your Majesty. We will do so, immediately. I will notify you once he is in Visitation Hall."

"Fine, you do that," grumbled Armbruster.

"What do you think about that, Yarlen? What happened to him? Who did this to the poor boy?"

"Sir, my guess is, it has something to do with the Queen. I am not trying to be disrespectful, but I believe it may have something to do with her plan."

"You are right, she is probably responsible. I sure would like to know why. I should confront her and ask."

"Sir, I do not think that is a good idea. I do not think we should let her know we are on to her plans."

"Once again, Yarlen, you are very wise. Thank you for thinking clearly when I cannot. My mind is confused. I miss my child. I am horrified by my wife's actions, and I am worried about her sister and Shawnatar."

"Sir, why don't you get some rest? I promise to inform you the minute they bring Collan. Shall I notify Essten?"

"No, absolutely not. Essten has been a loyal worker and friend. I will tell him later. Much later, after I rest a bit. Tell the others, no one is to say a word about Collan. Is that clear?"

"Yes, it is clear. I shall obey. I will ensure you are the one to announce his death."

Yarlen left the chamber and headed to his room. He had to conduct some research on spells that could be used on Alexis if need be. He was somber. This entire mess with Alexis was going to cause an outright war on Alstromia. He knew this was all part of her plan, to destroy Armbruster's leadership and subsequently allowing her to gain control over all of Alstromia.

Armbruster headed to his personal chamber. There, he sat on his bed, peering out the window. He saw pouring rain running down the window. He loathed rain. The thought depressed him further. He missed the sunshine and warmth on his face, wishing he was back on Earth with his friends. He loved and preferred the smells on Earth. He loved Earth's four seasons. He realized for the first time, he truly hated Alstromia. Alexis had ruined everything. Why was she doing this? Why could things not have just stayed the same? She could never have enough power. Alexis needed power to be happy and he had long ago realized she would do whatever it took to get it. Armbruster understood what was happening. He had lost his child and his wife, in one swift move. He closed his eyes. All he wanted to do was sleep. He did not want to think about anything else.

Yarlen opened the large, golden book. He flipped through the pages looking for something in particular. He scratched his head and retied the ribbon holding his hair in place. His beard itched. Everything was annoying him at the moment. He struggled to concentrate on the task at hand.

Halfway through the book, he stopped. He found what he had been looking for. A remarkable spell, the Spell of Insight. It would work better than any other. He looked at the long list of ingredients and wondered if they had those in the Tower. He shrugged his shoulders and made a list. He closed the book, placing it carefully back in its secret place.

He left the room on a mission to get the items he would need. The spell also required the assistance of two other Warlocks. He wondered if the others had been able to get the rest of the Guiders together to perform the spell to protect the planet. Oh well, he thought, no time to worry about that now. Time to focus on taking care of Alexis and the Spell of Insight, it took priority. He would let Armbruster sleep for now, no need to tell him anything. He would wait to speak with him. He needed rest to regain some power. He also needed to keep his mind off Alexis and the missing child. Best to just leave him alone, thought Yarlen, as walked to the Tower feeling empowered.

chapter 6

Revenge!

"Tell me where she is! I want to know right now!"

"You will NEVER see her again," laughed Loggane.

"You will surely perish. You realize this, Loggane. I am more powerful than you will ever be. Why fight this?" Alexis moved her Ceptre over his body and watched as the sparks made him squirm. "You really didn't think you would get away with this, did you? Silly, little warlock."

She hit Loggane in the stomach with her Ceptre. He wailed out in pain but grinned.

"You can do whatever you want to me, but you will never find her!" He smiled as he looked up at her, slightly wincing in pain.

"Tell me, where is she? I am losing my patience!" her face inches from his.

"You will never see your daughter again, Alexis! Trust me, she is forever gone," replied Loggane, an audacious smile on his face. It was all Alexis could take, she was done. No more games.

Alexis backed up and slammed her Ceptre into his head. Immediately, Loggane realized those would be the last words he would hear…ever! He faded away slowly…ever so slowly. His world became black. His eyes closed as blood gushed from his head, ending his life.

Alexis stood over him, watching as his life drained away. His hand twitched slightly and then stopped.

"I told you, you would die! I do not need you. I will find her on my own," asserted Alexis, looking at his lifeless body. She smiled, feeling powerful. He was not going to tell her what she needed. He was of no use, he had to die. Simple as that. She simply did what needed to be done. She walked out of the room, holding her blood-stained Ceptre high.

It had been easy to find Loggane, her spell had worked perfectly. She knew he was not smart enough to stop her. Alexis had found his whereabouts and expeditiously transported herself to his location. She knew beforehand, she would kill him. He would not tell her where he was hiding the child. It was not in his nature to be honest. Alexis was not worried about the fallout from her actions, she was in charge. No one would question her. She wanted to watch him suffer, withering in pain, as he had to succumbed to her power. She hoped it would not be a quick death, he did not deserve such kindness. Loggane should have to endure the same pain she felt at the loss of her daughter. She would remind him how it felt and make him realize he had made the worst mistake of his life.

Lorthana and Zandorah left the circle feeling empowered. They thanked the others for their help. Once at the top of the stairs, in the entry of the building, Lorthana cast a Homing Spell. Instantly, they appeared in Lorthana's home. Once in the sitting room, Zandorah looked at her mom with pride.

"I never knew you were so greatly respected."

"I was never a useless Witch, Zandi," replied Lorthana. Zandi was her nickname for Zandorah, even though Zandorah was not fond of the name.

"Mom, stop. I hate it when you call me Zandi, you know that. Please stop."

"Alright, my love, I will stop. Moms do that, they call their children by nicknames. I promise to try and control myself," she snickered.

Zandorah smiled. She really didn't hate it as much as she claimed, she just did not want her mother to know.

"Do you think we are okay? Do we need to worry?"

"I believe the spells have worked. I want to believe we are safe for now. Next, we need to find Alexis and Armbruster. I want to speak with Alexis."

"Mom, we cannot go to Alstromia. You know that."

"Yes, we can. I have a way. Trust me!"

"Okay, I will trust you, but I am scared. I am worried about Shawnatar."

"Everything will be okay. Shawnatar can take care of himself, no one will harm him. He is powerful and smart."

"Yes, Mom, but he is also still in love with Alexis, and that is not a good thing."

"He loves you, Zandi. Always has, always will. Believe that."

"He loves Alexis. He only married me to make her jealous. He talks in his sleep. He talks about her!"

"Oh, Zandi, I am so sorry, I did not know that."

"It's okay, Mom. I am used to it. I just thought, in time, he would forget her and let it all go. I wanted to believe he would love me."

"….and he will."

"No, he will not. I know that now."

"Well, let's not worry about that for the moment." Lorthana gently touched her daughter's hand. "Let's focus on what we need to do. We can worry about Shawnatar and Alexis some other time." She lovingly looked at her daughter. Zandorah nodded her head, but knew things would never be the same. Things had changed, the future even more uncertain.

Back at the Palace, Alexis sat in her chamber trying to figure out her next step. She ran both hands through her long hair, with her head tilted up, eyes closed. How could Loggane have been so awful? Why did he not tell her where to find her precious girl? What did he think he was going to accomplish by keeping it from her? She had been forced to end his insignificant life. There had been no turning back, he had sealed his own fate by his ignorance and stupidity.

She walked to the Eternal Mirror and stuck her head into it. She looked around hoping for a sign, any sign. The mirror only showed Armbruster conversing with his team. She could not hear what they were saying, but by their faces, she knew it was something not good. She pulled out of the mirror and brushed her hair. Why did the mirror always turn her hair ice cold? She really needed to find out more about this gift. It had been given to her as a wedding gift, by Armbruster's friend and confidant, Yarlen.

After she finished brushing her hair, she decided she was hungry and wanted to eat. She summoned Pershiah.

"Bring me something to eat and make it quick. I feel awful. Also, find Aerianna and tell her I want her in my chamber immediately. Do you hear me?" she shrieked at her assistant. Alexis had no patience for someone as slow as Pershiah. The girl moved at only one pace – slow.

"Yes, your Royal Highness, your wishes are my command. I will do so right away," replied Pershiah, as she bowed and ran from the room. She slammed the large door. Immediately, she opened it to apologize only to have Alexis scream at her to 'GET OUT!'

Alexis was in a foul mood. Where was Aerianna? She had expected Aerianna to be more aggressive in her search for answers. Yet, Aerianna had been gone for a long time. She had not yet reported back to Alexis. One thing was for sure, Alexis was sick and tired of all the crap. It seemed like she was the only one doing anything to move things along. Why was it always up to her to make things happen? Why did it seem like she was the only one able to reason and figure things out? It shouldn't be so damn complicated. Alexis sat despondent.

Down the hall, in her room, Aerianna finished reading more about the spell. She wanted to ensure she knew all the facts, good and bad, before she returned to Alexis. Not knowing all the facts would only irritate Alexis and cause more conflict. Just as she was about to put the book down, suddenly, there was a knock on her chamber door.

"Aerianna, Fanna of Alstromia, you have been summoned by her Majesty, Queen Alexis. She wishes your presence in her chamber at once." Pershiah closed the door and proceeded to the Food Chamber to prepare food for Alexis.

Aerianna lifted the book of spells off the table and decided to head to see Alexis, eager to speak with her. She was a bit nervous about what they were going to discuss. You never knew what kind of mood Alexis would be in. One moment she was happy as can be, the next she wanted you dead. It was best to be kind, quiet, and just listen most of the time.

"Your Majesty, it is Aerianna. May I enter?" she asked, as she knocked on the door.

"By all means, get in here!" Alexis responded in a huff. "What took you so long? I have been waiting." She looked at Aerianna annoyed. "You know how much I hate to wait." She tapped her fingers on her desk impatiently, making her point she was dissatisfied.

"I am so sorry, I came as soon as I was summoned. What can I do for you, Alexis?"

"Do for me? Nothing. It is what we must do. We must do many things. First, I have some tragic news to share with you. I must declare, Loggane is dead. He is gone." she blurted out, with a twisted smile on her face, causing Aerianna to frown.

"Uh, what exactly happened to Loggane? How do you know this?"

"Are you questioning me?" shouted Alexis, standing up, moving toward Aerianna with her Ceptre extended.

"No, of course not. I would never question you, my Queen. I was just asking if you know what had caused his death."

"My apologies, I am a bit on edge. Please, do not take this personally." She sarcastically smiled and sat down.

"So, what do you know, if I may ask?"

"It's all very simple. He kidnapped my daughter. He refused to tell me where she is and I ended his life. That's all," she flashed a wicked smile at Aerianna, instantly causing her to feel sick. What had Alexis done? Did Armbruster know she had done this? This action was permanent. There was no going back!

"Alexis, your Majesty – why did you do this?" inquired a mystified Aerianna.

"Were you not listening? I very clearly told you why," screamed an exasperated Alexis. "What part of 'he kidnapped my child' did you not understand? He was not going to give her back or tell me where she was, I had no choice." She got up and walked toward Aerianna. "Are you going to help me or not? This is your job, to be my Second in Command and not question me, or do you have a problem with this?" She tilted her head, awaiting a response. Aerianna looked at Alexis in shock. What was her problem? Had she lost her ever-loving mind?

"Alexis, I have always been by your side. You know I am here for you, no matter what. Of course, I am there for you…whatever you need."

"Okay then. Let's talk about how we are going to get my daughter back."

In the Food chamber, Pershiah prepared a feast for Alexis. She could have asked one of the other commoners to do so, but she wanted it done right. She placed all the food on a large silver platter, then on a Trillay - a type of cart. She whistled as she walked down the dark corridor, feeling good about the meal she had prepared.

Just as she was about to turn to walk down the Royal Hall, she stumbled into Pauto, Princess Lilah's security guard.

"Wow, Pershiah, what's the hurry? You almost ran me over with your Trillay. You really need to watch that corner," he joked and smiled, looking at Pershiah.

"I am so very sorry, Pauto. I did not see you. Are you okay?"

"No harm done, I am just on edge. Still looking for clues to find the Princess. We are on high alert and I am exhausted. I could use some food," he looked down at the platter on the Trillay and smiled.

"Oh no! That is for the Queen. I suggest you back away if you know what is good for you!" She grinned as she slapped his hand away from the Trillay. The two joked often with each other. He reached over and slightly patted her arm. "I would never. You better hurry and bring her the food or she will get angry. We all know what happens then," he shook his head and shrugged his shoulders.

Pershiah knew all too well what he meant. "Have a good night, Pauto." She pushed the Trillay on to the Queen's chamber. Pauto walked down the main corridor to find Yarlen and Armbruster.

Alexis fumed. "Where is that worthless girl? I am hungry. It should not take forever to make some food. I should have just used magic. I can never rely on her. She is unbelievable."

Just as Alexis was about to continue her rant, the door opened and Pershiah entered with the Trillay filled with food. "Your Majesty, I have brought your food," she announced proudly.

"Well, it is about time. What took you so long? You are the slowest witch I have ever met. I cannot rely on you, seriously!" Alexis walked toward the Trillay and looked at it with approval. She had to give Pershiah credit, she had made her favorites. Golden Fin Stew with crunchy bread, Vine of Blue in creamy sauce, and Chocolate, imported from Earth. She picked up the skinny, tall glass from the silver tray and took a whiff. It smelled like Porting Wine, a favorite on Alstromia, similar to wine on Earth but much sweeter. She looked happy. Alexis sat down next to the fireplace to enjoy her meal. Pershiah walked out of the room leaving Aerianna and Alexis alone.

"Mmmm, that does smell good. Enjoy your meal. I will leave you to it." Aerianna walked toward the door to leave.

"Excuse me! What are you doing? We are not done here. Just because I am eating does not mean our business is concluded for the night. Please sit down," she motioned for Aerianna to sit next to her on the short, white chair. Aerianna sat down quickly to comply.

"Okay, I am ready," announced Aerianna.

"Me too…," Alexis smiled as she took a sip of her Porting Wine, then swishing it around in her mouth. She was ready to find Loggane's accomplice, there had to be one. She intended to find whomever was part of this plot. It would be fun destroying them, the way she destroyed Loggane. Her evil grin grew as she looked at Aerianna.

chapter 7

Unknown

Marittaz held Essten's hand. She looked sweetly at him. He smiled, but noticed she quickly looked away. "What is wrong, my wife? Is there something you need to tell me?"

"Essten, I have heard some very disturbing news," Marittaz said releasing his hand and folding hers nervously. "You know, I went to the River of Miccay this afternoon to speak with some commoners about the Pearl Trade, right?"

"Yes, of course. You told me you were eager to get more pearls for the Torrins. Did something happen?" he asked apprehensively.

"Well, sort of. One of the older women told me how sorry she was for my loss. I was not sure what she meant, so I asked her to what she was referring. The woman looked confused and shook her head. She hugged me and started to cry. I pushed myself away and looked around to see the other women also looking sad, avoiding eye contact with me. The older woman put her hand on my shoulder and looked right at me and whispered: 'They pulled Collan from the river this morning. He is dead.' I almost fainted. It cannot be true."

"You foolish woman. Those women do not know what they are talking about. If Collan was dead, we would have been informed."

"I argued with her and said the same thing. The woman assured me that she saw his face when they pulled him onto the bank of the river. It was Collan, everyone at the river saw him. The Royal Guards took him back to the Palace."

"LIES! I do not believe it. If it were so, the King himself would have come to tell me, Armbruster would not keep that secret." Essten tried to convince himself as well as Marittaz. He had an uncomfortable feeling she was telling the truth.

"Essten, what if he is really dead?"

"Shut your mouth, woman. You are endangering our lives, there is always someone listening." He placed his pointer finger over his mouth, shaking his head. "I will not get tried for treason. I will not accuse our Queen or Armbruster of withholding this information! There is a logical explanation as to why we have not been informed, if it is true. I am telling you to shut up, be quiet! We are not going to discuss this here. I will go to the Palace to speak to Armbruster and find out about Collan. You, stay here. Do not, under any circumstances, talk to anyone. Have I made myself clear?" He gave her an annoyed look. She knew he was clearly warning her, realizing it was in her best interest to keep quiet.

"I am sorry, Essten. I am just so upset that it might be true. What if our Collan is dead? I am not sure how I can go on. Please forgive me," she began to sob. She put her head on the table and sobbed loudly. Essten got up from the table and walked to her side. He put his arms around her and gently rocked her, as he whispered into her ear: "I promise to find out about Collan. Do not worry."

Essten grabbed his patched, frayed, long robe and headed toward the stable. He unbuckled his Torrin and pulled back on the reigns. He flew high above the Valley of Grandu. Before he knew it, he found himself on the landing deck of the Palace. He handed the Torrin over to the Keeper. He smiled and reassured Essten he would take good care of his Torrin.

Essten stood before the massive arch leading to the entrance of the Palace, his hands sweaty. His stomach felt uneasy. He was certain of what he was about to hear. He had prepared himself from the moment Marittaz had informed him about Collan's possible death.

"Your Highness, Essten of the Valley of Grandu is here to see you," announced the commoner.

"See him into my chamber. I do not want to be disturbed," ordered Armbruster.

"Yes, your Highness."

Essten stared at the oversized, tan chairs by the fireplace. Ornate, Ozar candleholders graced the front of the fireplace, glowing with their Purple Flames of Passion. Obviously, Armbruster had some problems. He would not be burning these types of candles unless something was terribly wrong. It was customary to burn Purple Flames of Passion during times of stress. The scent from the candles provided calming effects.

"Sit down, my friend," requested Armbruster as he pointed to the chair on the left side of the fireplace.

"Thank you. How are you, Sir?"

"I am well. What brings you to the Palace, my friend? Did you find the white Torrin?"

"No, I came to ask you a question. I wanted to hear it from you," replied Essten.

Armbruster knew instantly what he meant. His heart skipped a beat, caught off guard. He was not prepared to tell Essten about Collan.

"What is it, my friend? What may I do for you?" he asked, pretending not to know.

"Tell me, is it true? Did your guards find my son in the River of Miccay today? Is he truly dead? Please, do not lie to me!" begged Essten, tears welling up in his eyes.

Armbruster got up from his chair and paced around in front of Essten. He stopped in front of Essten and simply shook his head. Essten instantly realized Armbruster had known.

"Look, I was going to tell you later today. My guards were trying to clean up his body. We planned to put his body in Visitation Hall, then inform you about his passing. I did not want you to see him in the condition he was brought to the Palace. I know you want to see him."

"Sir, did your guards find out what happened?"

"No, we do not yet know. I have every guard trying to get information. I will not rest until we find out something, I promise! You have my word."

"Sir, I just want to see my boy. Please!"

"Very well. I will have one of my guards take you to Visitation Hall."

"Thank you, you are very kind. I appreciate all you do for me and my family. Please, forgive me," he started to cry. Armbruster pulled Essten close and gave him a hug. He could only imagine how much this man was hurting. What a tragic loss, his only child.

After a short time, Essten backed away. "I am so sorry, your Majesty. That will never happen again."

"Essten, never apologize for loving your child. I am only sorry I had to tell you. My heart breaks for you."

Armbruster ordered the guard outside his door to take Essten to Visitation Hall. Meanwhile, he would look for Alexis. He wanted to find out what she was doing and why she did not show up for dinner.

Thunder rumbled outside as Alexis sat in the chamber next to Aerianna, staring out the large window. Alexis glanced at Aerianna, her eyes squinting in such a way wishing for her to speak. Aerianna had very little to say. Alexis wanted to scream, but chose to keep her thoughts to herself and continued to look outside. She could see Trimbers sway in the wind as lightning flashed. She grinned. She loved the eerie weather, happy there was no sunshine to be found on this planet. She adored the rain, the howling wind, and the bright flashes of lightning. It reminded her of power, strong and bold!

"What do you want to do next, Alexis? We need to talk with Armbruster about Loggane. He has a right to know."

"Have you lost your mind? I am not telling Armbruster about Loggane. Not yet, anyway. The last thing I need is him accusing me of… acting out of spite. I had every right to take his life. He took my child, he had to die. Armbruster will not understand. He was close to Loggane and it will not be a good day when I must tell him. Come to think of it, I will not be telling him. That's the end of it. Stop bringing it up."

Alexis stood up and walked to the fireplace. She placed her hands on her hips as he looked deeply into the fire. She tilted her head back and looked up to the ceiling. She let out a long sigh and spun around. Aerianna looked confounded.

"What is it?"

"I am at a complete loss," declared Alexis.

"And why do you feel that way? I thought we knew what we were going to be doing next?"

"I am talking about Armbruster. I am at a total loss, as to what to say to him, and what to do about him. I am starting to think he is more than just an inconvenience. He is asking too many questions and causing too many issues."

"What are you saying, Alexis?" asked Aerianna with a look of uncertainty.

"You know exactly what I am saying, Aerianna. He has to be dealt with, one way or another. He can either become a game player or he will be taken out. He is a liability."

"Wow, I did not realize you hated him so much."

"I never said I hated him. I said, he was becoming a liability. If he is not working with me, then he is working against me. Those working against me, will be taken care of accordingly. I do not have the time for indecisiveness. Yarlen is probably already looking into spells to help Armbruster. We must be smarter and quicker than both. Am I making myself clear?"

Alexis looked at Aerianna waiting for a sign of approval. Instead, Aerianna looked down and avoided eye contact with Alexis. This only seemed to make Alexis angrier. She tapped her Ceptre on the table with frustration, staring directly at Aerianna.

"Wake up, silly girl. You took a vow to protect me, be by my side, and help me any way you can. Now, you simply look away? Must I now question your loyalty, too?"

"Never! I agree. We will do what we must," declared a nervous Aerianna.

"Good. For a second, I felt rather unhinged. I would hate to think we were not on the same team. Never let me question your loyalty again, do you understand me? Friend or not, I cannot have betrayal in my inner circle."

"You have my loyalty and my life. I promise."

"Tell me about the spells you have found and what you think we should do next. I also want an update on Zandorah, Shawnatar, and Lorthana. Who is looking into the activities on Earth?"

"I do not have all the answers to these questions, but I promise I will look into it and get back to you as soon as I know. May I go forth?"

"Oh, I suppose. When you do return, be prepared. I want both spells and the answers about my sister, my mother, and Shawnatar. Understood? I am getting tired of repeating myself. I really thought you were more capable than this." Alexis looked at Aerianna with displeasure. Why was this girl turning out to be such a problem? She was supposed to be her Second in Command and a leader, she was acting more like a follower.

"I will not fail you, my Majesty. I promise." Aerianna stood up and ran out of the chamber. She felt her heart beating fast in her chest. She knew she had failed Alexis, and Alexis was beyond upset. She would need to make it up to Alexis and regain her trust before she would be faced with severe consequences. No one liked the consequences.

Alexis watched as Aerianna ran from the chamber like a coward. She hated it. She hated what her best friend and confidant had become. What was going on? Was Alexis the only one with common sense? She needed to regain control. Alexis shrugged her shoulders and walked to the window. She flung herself into her favorite chair. She picked up her book on the table and read out loud: *"No one is going to hand it to you. Make it happen."* Hmmm, Earthly wisdom. She had kept the book from an Earth-dwelling friend, Shell. Shell had been the most amazing human. She knew exactly who and what Alexis was, but loved her still the same. Alexis missed Shell more than she wanted to admit. Shell had once told Alexis she would love to go to Alstromia with her, but knew Alexis would not allow it. Humans and witches did not mix, it was frowned upon. Alexis would not jeopardize her status by allowing a human to enter Alstromia.

Alexis reminisced about a cool spring day, a long time ago, when she first met Shell. She had been by the river in New England, walking and looking for some wild herbs. As she squatted down to pick up a few mushrooms, she heard a noise. She spun around to see a petite, blonde woman staring at her. The woman moved in close to her to introduced herself.

"Hi, I am Shell. I did not mean to scare you. I was out looking for my dog, Clark. Have you seen him? He is a golden retriever wearing a red collar."

"Ummm, no. I have not seen anyone… other than you, that is."

"Oh, okay. Are you lost? No one ever comes out here. I was surprised to see anyone else."

"I live nearby. I was just out looking for some wild herbs, berries, and mushrooms."

"I see….so, what is your name?"

"Oh, I am so sorry. So very rude of me. I am Alexis."

"Pleasure to meet you."

"Well, I best be on my way. I hope you find your dog. It is going to get dark soon."

"Yes, I know. I hope I find him too. Maybe we meet again some time?"

"You never know. See you later, Shell." Alexis had walked off and smiled. She liked something about Shell. As she stood next to her, she felt an odd but comfortable bond with her. It confused Alexis. Over time, they became great friends. Leaving Shell on Earth was one of the most difficult decisions of her life. Her heart ached and felt incomplete. Shell was probably one of the only people who really knew the real Alexis. Thinking about Shell made her smile, but sad at the same time.

Alexis wondered about Shell. Where was she? Did she still think about Alexis? Thoughts turned to frustration. Alexis shook her head and tried to erase all thoughts of Shell. Why had she come back into her mind? Maybe Aerienna's lack of support drove her to think about Shell, the one person she knew would never betray her. Yet, she had left her on Earth.

A loud knock on the door caused Alexis to come back to reality. She blinked and screamed "what is it?"

Armbruster forced open the massive chamber door and walked in. He looked old and drawn. His hair looked frizzy and his robe looked dirty. Obviously, Armbruster lacked proper personal hygiene and sleep.

"What are you doing?" she interrogated. It was way too late for this, she thought. She was tired and upset. She wanted to sleep.

"Alexis, we need to talk." He looked at her seriously and stepped aside. Yarlen jumped out from behind Armbruster. He quickly smacked her in the head with his Ceptre. Before she had a chance to say anything, Yarlen chanted the Spell of Return. She felt her head become light as air. She felt a stabbing pain so strong, she wanted to throw up. Within seconds, she fell to the ground and became unconscious. Her limp body was face down in the fluffy rug by the fireplace.

Armbruster dropped to his knees to roll her over. She had blood running down her head.

"What did you do? Are you insane? I did not tell you to kill her!"

"Relax, your Majesty. She will be fine."

"What is happening?" shrieked Armbruster as he looked at his wife, fading away, turning into a ghostly apparition. He tried to touch her, only to have her fall through his hands, like sand…

"She is returning…it is as I planned."

chapter 8

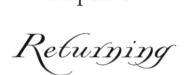

Armbruster looked at Yarlen, horrified. What had he done? Could it be undone?

"Yarlen, you must explain." He looked down at the ghostly appearance of his wife. She floated above the ground, hair waving gently from side to side. Her entire being an icy, blue-gray color, looking like a beautiful ghost. Her eyes were closed and hands dangling limp by her side.

"Sir, I did what had to be done. We had to stop her. You are now back in control. It was what you wanted, no?" Yarlen asked nervously. He thought Armbruster would say something like 'great job, my friend' or 'finally'...instead he seemed upset. What should he say? What should he do? Yarlen was shocked.

"Have you lost your mind? Of course, I am upset. Look at that!" He pointed to Alexis, or what used to be Alexis. "You better tell me you can reverse this. I may not be happy with her right now, but this...this is out of control! Do you hear me?"

"Armbruster, your Majesty, I am sorry. I was under the impression you wanted this. I really thought you wanted her out of the way and this was the only way to do that. She is, or was, so strong. It would have been difficult to control her otherwise. I searched through all the books, this was the best solution for our situation."

"You are avoiding the point. Is it reversible?" Armbruster looked directly at Yarlen, angrier than he had been in a long time.

Nervously, Yarlen looked away and started marching around the room in a circle. He was not looking at Armbruster or Alexis. He was not sure what to say or do. He had not really thought about it as being a 'reversible spell,' he assumed it would be permanent. It had been his first thought to get rid of Alexis, to help Armbruster regain control, and to put him back in charge. This seemed like the most logical way to accomplish that. He spun around and walked toward Armbruster.

"Sir, I really do not know. That is my answer. I am not sure we can reverse her condition! I assumed this was in the best interest of our clan and our new Order, I was doing what I thought was best. I thought you would be okay with it, especially since she attempted to betray you. You were so upset with her. You wanted to 'kill her' so I just assumed you wanted me to stop her….no matter how. That is exactly what I did. I did this for you. I am so very sorry you are mad and upset. I thought you would be pleased."

Armbruster tried to remain calm. He shook his head, wrung his hands, and brushed his hands through his hair. He looked at Yarlen in disbelief. Had he heard him correctly? Had he just stated Alexis could be like this forever? Oh, no, that was not going to happen. She was still his wife, he still loved her, and he wanted her back.

He walked up next to Yarlen. "May I be frank?" he asked with a scowl on his face.

"Of course, your Majesty."

"If you do not find a way to reverse this spell, I will do everything in my power to make you suffer the most awful death! DO YOU UNDERSTAND ME?" he screamed.

Yarlen started shaking, almost in a convulsive way. His eyes began to roll in the back of his head, mouth foaming. He dropped to the ground screaming out in pain, withering on the ground, unable to breathe.

Armbruster stood over him chanting, his voice slowing increasing, as did the pain for Yarlen. He allowed the pain to go on for a short while. Then, he walked to the chair and sat down. From there, Armbruster watched as Yarlen picked himself off the floor and stood up, his legs visibly shaking. He used his Ceptre as a cane to stand. He slowly managed to make it to the door and turned to look at Armbruster.

"I will find a reversal, I promise. Leave her where she is. I will be back." He limped out the door slowly. He slithered down the hall as quickly as he could, considering his legs felt numb.

Armbruster looked at Alexis floating above the floor, looking ghostly. He could not believe what had happened. How did he make Yarlen believe he wanted this? He never wanted to seriously hurt Alexis, he just wanted her to obey and be a loving, caring, wife and mother. He looked at her body, swaying lightly. She looked so peaceful and beautiful. She was a stunningly gorgeous witch. He continued to observe her from the seat, but felt compelled to walk to her side. Once standing over her, he looked down and gazed at her with feelings of love. As he was about to go back to the chair, he felt a sharp, cold pain in his leg. He looked down to see her ghostly hand in his leg, producing the pain he felt. She seemed 'awake' and her eyes were wide open. She looked crazy, wild, and mad. All of a sudden, he was scared.

Alexis felt the pain for a small second, and then, only felt her head become light. It felt like a balloon and not at all like her body. She noticed her arms and legs had become paralyzed, dangling like lifeless pieces of flesh. Her eyes would not open. She could hear voices in the background, presumably Yarlen and Armbruster. What had transpired? Had Yarlen killed her? Was she dead? Why could she not open her eyes? She heard Armbruster speaking in an agitated voice.

"Have you lost your mind? Of course, I am upset. Look at that!"

Was he talking about her? What did that mean?

"You better tell me you can reverse this. I may not be happy with her right now but this...this is out of control! Do you hear me?"

Helllooo, I am right here! Why was nobody listening to me? They were talking as if she was not there? Her head hurt badly. She felt cold. She wished she could crawl into her warm bed and have a nice, warm fire in her fireplace. Hmmm, why was she so cold?

"Armbruster, your Majesty, I am sorry. I was under the impression you wanted this. I really thought you wanted her out of the way and this was the only way to do that."

Blah, blah, blah…whatever! Okay, you thought you could get rid of me, I get it, Alexis thought. She listened to their conversation, still unable to move or open her eyes. Slowly, she felt her hands move a bit more, her feet wiggling, her head moving. Hmmm, maybe she will wake up and all this is a bad dream? She could not imagine this being the end. No, this was not how she would go out permanently, no way! She heard Yarlen leave and then there was silence in the room. She quietly whispered "come to me my love" hoping Armbruster would hear her. It seemed like an eternity, then suddenly he was standing over her. She could feel his presence. She tried to move her arm to reach for his leg. She felt something. Suddenly, she felt him move. She opened her eyes. He stared straight down at her face. She knew at that instance, he was not standing over her to protect her, rather he was trying to figure out if this was the best way for her to spend the rest of her life. She was not going to let that happen. She would have to find a way to stop all of this, and then focus on getting her daughter back.

Aerianna woke up very early. She had spent most of the night trying to find some spells to beat Yarlen. She did not want Alexis upset with her again. There was no way she was going to let her down. Aerianna would prove herself to Alexis and gain back her trust. She walked over to her window and pulled back the heavy, velvet curtains imported from Earth. She looked out and it was still raining. She missed the sunshine. Alexis liked things gloomy. The dreary environment depressed Aerianna.

The rest of the clan liked the weather similar to Earth. Most of them had become accustomed to Earth's weather and changing seasons. It was nice being able to see snow falling out of the sky, then experiencing the warmth of the sun. She missed Earth. At first, it had been great on Alstromia. Alexis had allowed the weather conditions to stay as they had been, similar to Earth. Once she had made changes, many were displeased about the atmosphere and weather. It was dreary and cold most of the time.

Aerianna walked to her wardrobe and picked out some clean clothes to wear. She put on her dark, purple robe. She felt most comfortable in it. She slipped on her matching slippers and picked up her book of Spells. She waved her Ceptre over the bed and ensured it was made and tidy. She aimed the Ceptre at the fireplace to start a fire, it was so cold in the chamber room. She left the room to head to the library to see if Alexis was there researching spells.

Yarlen was snoring in the large chair in the corner of the library. He had little drops of drool dripping off his chin. He had been hurting and felt extremely exhausted when he fell asleep. He felt a pulling motion on his arm that startled him. His eyes fluttered open. He tried to focus on the blurry face that appeared. Someone handed him his reading glasses. He gently placed them on his nose, he looked up, and smiled.

"Thank you, Aerianna. I appreciate it. I guess I fell asleep."

"Oh yeah, you were snoring away. You must have really been tired. Why did you not go to your chamber? Are you okay?"

"Yes, I am fine. Why do you ask?"

"It looks like you have black eyes, they are swollen and very dark. Are you sure you are okay?"

"I will be fine. No need to worry, child."

"Okay, if you say so. What are you doing here? Anything special?"

"I was researching some reversal spells for a project. I have not been able to find one that will work though. I need it immediately. It is very important," explained Yarlen, attempting to remain vague.

"What kind of reversal spell? Can you tell me? Maybe I can be of assistance?" asked a curious Aerianna.

"No, I cannot say…sorry."

"Oh…okay. Well, if you change your mind, let me know."

"I will." He picked up his books and walked out of the library. The last thing he needed was Aerianna asking questions, that would only complete things. He would find Armbruster and tell him about his run-in with Aerianna.

Aerianna sat in the chair and leaned back as she watched Yarlen walk out of the library. Very suspicious, she thought. Something was wrong, he was acting very odd. What was going on here? What kind of a reversal spell? Why would he need to reverse something? What had he done? She better find Alexis and tell her about this right away.

Essten walked up to the concrete table in the massive Visitation Hall Chamber. There was the lifeless body of his only son, Collan. The lower half of his body draped in a purple and gold blanket – the Death Sheet, as it was called. As he approached the table, he felt weak in the knees. He saw his son's face, almost unrecognizable. Deep lacerations and scratches on his face looked as though he had been dragged along the riverbank. His entire face was black, blue, and swelling was extensive. His eyes were forced shut by the excessive swelling. His bottom lip, split open. Essten saw one of his teeth sticking out. It was a dreadful scene. He cried as he looked at his son. What a waste of a life. How did this happen? Who had done this to his son and why? He placed his head on his son's chest and wept. Essten was grateful Armbruster had his body cleaned up. He was glad he had not seen it before, this was bad enough.

Deep in the chambers of the dungeon, Aerianna hid two books she had found in the library. She did not want Yarlen or anyone else to find them. They had been on the top shelf in the ElderWize section. It was the section containing the oldest and best spells. The black book of spells was falling apart, but most of the inside was still legible. She wanted to see if she could find anything extraordinary, hoping to impress Alexis.

Once the books were safely tucked away in her special hiding spot, she closed the door to the dungeon chamber room and locked it. She put the gold key in the inside pocket of her robe. She ran up the long, winding, stone stairway to the main floor. At the top, she glanced around the corner, ensuring no one was around before she came up the stairs. She did not want anyone to see her appear from the dungeons, it would most likely raise suspicion. She did not need that aggravation.

No one was around. She walked up the last step and turned the corner. She headed to the west wing, toward Alexis' chamber. She stood in front of the door and knocked. She waited, but there was no response. She knocked again. She attempted to turn the old, oval knob. Nothing. It did not move and appeared to be locked. She knocked again.

"Go away! We are sleeping," yelled Armbruster.

Shocked, Aerianna jumped back from the door in disbelief. Did he just say 'we are sleeping?' Ummm, since when was he allowed in her chamber? It had been months, nine or ten months to be exact.

"Sir, I need to speak with the Queen."

"I said GO AWAY. We are sleeping and do not want to be disturbed."

"Yes, your Majesty. I am so sorry." She walked away, wondering why Armbruster was in the chamber with Alexis, claiming to be sleeping.

Armbruster rolled onto his back. He glanced at Alexis. She

floated next to him on the bed, either sleeping or her eyes were just closed. He sighed.

"Alexis, are you sleeping?" he asked

There was no response. He looked closely at her.

"Alexis, answer me, please!" he begged.

"Go away, Armbruster. You did this. Look at me!"

She spoke! He did not know if he should be happy or worried.

"Now, honey…it will be okay, I promise."

"Now, honey? Seriously? This is far from okay," snarled Alexis.

Armbruster smirked. He was actually finding this to be sort of funny. She seemed so harmless in this condition, and for the first time in months, this was a comfortable situation for him. His smile widened. She noticed the smile and tried to slap his face, but her hand passed right through his face. Annoyed, she tried again. This time, he felt a sharp pain radiate through his cheek. She smiled the moment she saw him wince. Theirs was truly a love/hate relationship. She started to laugh and so did he. The two laughed, then stopped abruptly when there was another knock at the door.

"Your Majesty, we need to speak with you, immediately. We have news!"

"I will be right out, Pauto."

"Alexis, stay here, and do not answer the door. I will be back."

"Where would I go like this?" she snidely remarked.

He smiled. "Yes, I suppose you are right. I will be back soon."

He got up and walked to the door. He closed the door, and on the way out, locked it from the outside.

Alone in the room, Alexis looked up at the ceiling as she floated over the bed. She tried to move or sit up and could not. How could she learn to maneuver in this state? This was beyond frustrating. She did not like being in this state, not being able to move around freely. She closed her eyes and tried to visualize moving toward the chair. Nothing. She hovered over the bed, wanting to scream. Why was this not working? She shook her head. Move already, she told herself. She forced herself to move. Slowly, she managed to get herself in an upright position. She had done it! She hovered over the chair and pretended to be seated. She looked at the fireplace. What was Armbruster up to? Where was that worthless girl, Aerianna? Why did she not come back after Armbruster left? She could only assume what Aerianna was thinking about when Armbruster claimed to be sleeping in her chamber. Alexis wanted to laugh.

Down the hall, Aerianna walked slowly toward her room. She was completely taken back by the fact Armbruster was in the Queen's room. How was that possible? They had stopped being together after Lilah was conceived. Since then, they lived separate lives. Maybe they were back together again? Wait! Something occurred to her. Why had Alexis not spoken when she knocked on the door? Why had Armbruster replied and there had been no sound from Alexis? There was something wrong. Alexis would never have allowed it. She would have said something to Aerianna. Alexis would not have given Armbruster the permission to speak on her behalf.

Aerianna turned around and ran back to the Queen's chamber. Once she approached the door, she gently knocked three times. She waited for Armbruster to yell. There was no response. She knocked more loudly this time and announced her presence.

"Your Majesty, it is Aerianna. May I enter?"

"Enter, you silly girl."

Aerianna turned the handle, only to find out it was locked.

"It is locked. Can you please unlock it?"

"Armbruster locked it on his way out. Why don't you cast a spell to unlock it? Gosh, stop being so useless!" responded Alexis.

"Yes, Alexis!" Aerianna raised her Ceptre and chanted. She could hear the lock make a clanking noise. She turned the handle and opened the door. Before she could open the door all the way, Alexis yelled at her.

"Wait! Before you enter, I have to tell you something. Please, do not be afraid."

"Umm, why would I be afraid, your Majesty? May I enter?"

"Only if you promise not to scream."

"Okay, you are scaring me." She gently pushed the door open the rest of the way. She turned around and closed the door behind her, then turned to face Alexis. She stared straight ahead. What she saw utterly confused her. She shook her head and backed up. What is that?

"I do not understand," said Aerianna in a whisper-quiet tone, eyes large in disbelief.

"Yes, thank Yarlen for this one. I believe he used a Return Spell on me, also known as the dreaded 'Ghosting' spell. Stop staring at me, for goodness sake. I am not dead. I am just…. sort of not here. Yes, I am here in mind and spirit. Ha-ha, get it…spirit." She started laughing, thinking it was very funny. She looked at Aerianna. She looked scared, far from amused.

"Alexis, this is not funny! Can this be reversed? I thought the Ghosting Spell or the Return Spell was permanent? Tell me it is not. This is awful." Aerianna's eyes welled up with tears. She looked away. Her friend, the Queen, a dreaded ghost-like figure. This was awful.

"Stop it, silly girl. I will be fine. I know there are spells that can reverse it. The question is, can the idiot find it in time?"

"What do you mean by 'in time'?"

"Welllll, most of the time, the Ghosting Spell has to be reversed in two Earthly days or it will become permanent. Yarlen better hurry up, quite a lot of time has already passed and the clock is ticking, so to speak."

"Are you serious?" screamed a scared and distraught Aerianna.

"Calm down. Yes, I am very serious."

"Well then, what would keep him from reversing it? Maybe

he wants you to stay this way? Maybe Armbruster likes you as his new, ghostly wife. Have you thought of that?"

"Okay, you seriously need to relax a bit. Armbruster does not want the mother of his child, or his wife, to be a ghost. What kind of life would that be? Also, once we find our precious daughter, I need to be able to raise her properly. Armbruster knows that all too well. He is not crazy. Sometimes, he is a bit impulsive, but never, would he want to harm me. This I know for sure!"

"If you say so, my Queen."

Aerianna walked closer to Alexis. "May I touch you?"

"Why?"

"Curiosity."

"Oh my gosh, whatever." She extended her hand toward Aerianna. Aerianna touched her gently. Her hand felt like a shard of ice, sharp and cold. She impulsively pulled back her hand from the pain.

"Wow, that hurt. So cold. Does it hurt?"

"Listen up. Enough. Yes, I feel cold. Yes, it is not fun. Yes, I hate it. Let's move on. We have more pressing matters to attend to. I need you to go to the Tullah Mountain and find Florenzzah, she will help you figure out a way to reverse this thing. I do not want to leave it up to Yarlen. He may be good, but he is old and very slow. I do not have time to wait. Time is definitely not on my side. If you have ever wanted to prove yourself to me, now is the time."

"Yes, your Majesty. I will go see her immediately. I will return as quickly as I can. Is there anything I can do for you in the meantime?"

"Not unless you can give me back my body?" whispered Alexis, to herself.

"Did you say something, my Queen?"

"Yes, hurry up you lazy girl, get moving!"

Aerianna bowed her head and walked out of the chamber. She ran to her room to gather her bag. Once she entered her room, she walked to the shelf and pulled the bag down from rickety, old bookshelf by the door. She proceeded to fill it with a few items she thought would be useful for trade. Witches always expected something in exchange for something, nothing was free. Confidently, she left the room and walked down the corridor toward the landing pad. There, she asked the Keeper to retrieve her Torrin.

Once on the Torrin, she steered her Torrin in the direction of Tullah Mountain. She loved to fly. She loved the feel of the brisk air in her hair, as well as the view from above, looking down at the village below. Huts of commoners lined the river bank. The wealthier commoners were fortunate to own a mini compound, comprised of several huts, sitting side by side. She looked at the twin moons. The moons, a bright whitish-gray at night, tried desperately to peek through the cloud cover. Unlike Earth, there was no sun, the days defined by the color of the moons. During the day, they were a very bright teal color.

She could have used magic to teleport herself to Tullah Mountain, however, she enjoyed the time flying. Flying gave her time to think. She had a lot to think about and wanted to clear her head before she faced Florenzzah.

chapter 9
Unexpected Surprises

"She is such a stunning child, don't you think?"

"Oh yes, she certainly is. I just wish we did not have her here. I do not want to get caught watching this baby. If the Queen finds out we are watching her child, she will surely kill us both," said Shell.

"Stop saying things like that. No one knows she is on Earth, all is well. No one would suspect she is with humans."

"Alexis knows everything. She has her spies here on Earth. It is only a matter of time before someone figures it all out."

"No one will ever suspect. Everyone believes you gave birth to this child, no one knows our child was stillborn. Our secret is safe, as is the princess," declared Joran.

"This is one debt I wish was paid. I do not like this, not at all. I hate having to lie to our family and friends. I worry about the end result. How will this end? I assume, badly!"

"Time will tell. Stop worrying, Shell. You are doing this to save the child and help your best friend."

"I hope you are right, I really do. It feels like betrayal, and I know that Alexis will not tolerate that. She will have her revenge. The last thing I ever want to do is to hurt her," said Shell sadly.

"You are a good and loyal friend. I know this has been difficult. However, look at that child. This was the best thing we could have done to help Alexis, we saved them both from someone vengeful. In time, you will see this was the best decision. You will learn to accept it. Let us not worry about it for now. We must ensure the safety of the child, that is our priority. We absolutely have to do this!"

"I know you are right. It just feels so wrong," professed Shell.

"Rest assured…you are strong and making the right choice. Stop second guessing our decision. Remember the purpose behind the plan," said Joran as he lovingly looked at his wife.

"I love you, Joran. You are right. I just never wanted to hurt or disappoint Alexis."

"I love you, too. Now, chin up. Smile. Let's put 'our' baby to bed. Let us relax and enjoy this glorious, fall day."

They gently placed Lilah in the crib and closed the door. They walked, holding hands, back to the living room. There, Joran opened the back door. They stepped onto the back patio and sat down on the rickety, wooden deck chairs, looking at the mountains. Shades of orange, red, and yellow blended together to form trees. It was a beautiful day. A crisp, light breeze brought shivers to Shell. She wrapped her shawl more tightly around herself. She looked off into the distance thinking about Alexis, wondering how she was doing without her precious child. Leaves fell from the tree next to her. She watched as they gently landed on the ground. She stared at the leaves for a minute thinking. A hard grip brought her thoughts back to reality.

"Shell, we need to get inside. NOW."

"What is it, Joran?" asked Shell looking all around nervously.

"There, look! Off in the distance, on the right," he pointed to a dark cloud. It seemed to hover over the lake. How odd.

Joran grabbed Shell by the arm and pulled her into the house. He closed and locked the door. He closed the shades to all the windows as well. He motioned for her to sit on the sofa by the fireplace. He placed his finger over his mouth, telling her to be quiet.

She looked at him and shook her head, not understanding what was happening. He walked over to her and whispered in her ear.

"Go see Lilah. Do not make a sound, no matter what you hear. I think they have found us. Go quietly…and swiftly. I love you!"

He pushed her toward the door to the nursery. He watched, as she walked into the room and closed the door. He walked, cautiously, to the window by the kitchen, peeking through the blinds to see what was happening outside. He saw the cloud had turned a purple-gray color and it was closer than before. The sky had turned darker, too. The wind had picked up, leaves were hitting the window rapidly. He heard branches scratching the side of the house from the massive oak tree by the living room. He remembered, he was supposed to have trimmed back the branches which he had forgotten to do.

Lilah was sleeping on her side, suckling her thumb. She was unaware of what was happening outside. Shell watched over her nervously. She walked to the door and listened for any noises. She heard nothing. Scared, she walked back to the crib and rubbed Lilah's back. Shell was feeling sick to her stomach. She could not think, she could barely breathe. She turned to walk softly to the window and attempted to peek out. Lifting one of the slats of the wooden blinds, she saw it had started raining. She could not see the dark cloud they had spotted earlier by the lake, unaware it now over the house. Shell turned away from the window and walked to the rocking chair. There, she sat down, staring at the crib. She pulled the blanket over her lap and covered up. She shivered. It was extremely cold in the room and she was scared. She wondered what was going on in the room with Joran. Was he okay?

In the other room, Joran watched as the cloud moved over the house. The rain was loudly pounding the metal roof and making a clunking noise. He looked over to the other side of the room, at the enormous wall in the living room. He noticed the fire in the fireplace had died. He walked to the fireplace and lit three of the candles on the mantle. The room had become very dark. He threw a large log onto the dying flames, hoping it would reignite the fire. For added measure, he crumpled up some paper and added it to the fire, attempting to accelerate the flames. Within a minute, the flames grew tall and the fire seemed to have caught. He walked to the nursery and quietly opened the door.

He saw Shell curled up in the chair, sleeping with a blanket. In the crib, Lilah appeared to be sleeping too. He closed the door and walked back to the living room. He gazed out the large window to see if he could still spot the cloud. Just as he was about to open the curtain a bit more, a bright light hit his face. It was so bright and blinding. He fell backwards and tripped. He hit his head on the table, falling onto the rug by the sofa. Panicking, he managed to look up. That is when he saw her. He wanted to speak, but his eyes felt heavy. He succumbed to the pain. He closed his eyes before he could speak.

A woman entered the room alone. She held her massive Ceptre out in front and used her Bright Spell to blind Joran. She did not plan on him hitting his head or causing his fall. She bent over and checked on him. His chest is moving…he is still breathing, good! She never meant for any of this to happen. Where was the child? Where was Shell? She left the room to find them.

The first room she encountered was empty, nothing in the room to indicate life. She closed the door and moved to the next room. It was another bedroom. It, too, was completely empty. She was getting tired of this. She proceeded to the next room, opened the door, and smiled. There, Shell was curled up in a chair sleeping, a gentle snoring coming from her. She glanced over to the other side of the room and saw the crib. She walked quietly to the crib and looked down. Princess Lilah was curled up on her side, her thumb in her mouth, sleeping peacefully. She bent down over the crib and picked up the sleeping Princess, wrapped up in a tiny cloak. Once she held the child firmly in her arms, she banged her Ceptre firmly on the floor and they both disappeared.

"Joran, is that you?" Shell looked around confused. She turned on the light and looked around. She walked to the crib. Where was Lilah? She frantically ran to the living room. There, she saw Joran on the rug, passed out. She ran to him. In a frenzy, she started shaking him, hoping he was still alive.

"Are you okay? Please, please, be okay!" she cried. She listened to his chest and could hear him breathing.

"I hear you. Stop shaking me, my head hurts," grumbled Joran. His head pounded and his arm was hurting from her pulling on it so much.

"Thank goodness you are okay. Where is Lilah? Did you hide her?"

"What are you saying, woman? I do not have her. She was with you, in her crib." He sat up and rubbed his head. He had a massive lump on the side of his skull. No blood though – that was fortunate.

"I assumed you took her when I was sleeping. I woke up and she was gone!"

"WHAT! What do you mean gone?"

"She is not in the crib; the room is empty!"

"We are in trouble." He rubbed his head and rolled his eyes. He looked at Shell. She sat on the edge of the couch looking at him in disbelief, looking terrified. He managed to sit up and squinted his eyes. His neck hurt.

"What are we going to do?"

"Do? Nothing. We need to sit here and figure out our next step. You need to get in touch with your sister."

"Yes!"

chapter 10

The Calm before the Storm

"Mom, let me hold her, please!"

"Okay, here you go. Hold her gently." Lorthana handed the baby to Zandorah.

"She really does look like Alexis. She is gorgeous. Are we going to give her back to Alexis now?" asked Zandorah.

"No, not yet. We need to find out who originally kidnapped her. I am just glad our clan found the baby. I knew if we put out the word, someone would find her."

"What should we do next?"

"I think we need to find a place to hide her, temporarily. We must get ahold of Shawnatar and tell him we are okay, he will be worried," said Lorthana, looking at her daughter with a concerned smile. She knew Zandorah would want Shawnatar to know they were okay. She also knew Zandorah felt guilty.

"Mom, stop! I do not want to discuss him." She turned to walk out the door.

"Where are you going?"

"Going to the kitchen to make something to eat. I need to think about how we are going to keep Lilah safe. We, ourselves, are in great danger. Mom, we are in trouble." She walked out of the room angry, with her lips pursed.

Lorthana held Lilah and smiled. The child was sleeping and

looked so beautiful. She held her close to her chest and rocked her, breathing in her smell. Baby smell, she thought. So sweet and innocent. Lorthana thought about what Zandorah had said. She was right, they were all in grave danger. How would they explain the presence of the child? What would Alexis do if she found out they had Lilah? How would they be able to reunite the child with her parents without endangering their own lives?

Frustrated, she gently placed the child in the middle of the chair by the fireplace. She walked to the window to look outside. She could hear noises coming from the kitchen. Obviously, Zandorah was upset. She was making a lot of noise while preparing the food. Pots, pans and dishes made pinging noises, cupboard doors slamming. Zandorah was having a heated conversation by herself, loud enough so Lorthana could understand some of the words.

In the kitchen, Zandorah slammed down jars of food from the cupboard. She was frustrated and angry. How in the world could Lorthana remain so calm after what they had done?

She prepared a simple meal and placed it on the small, oval table by the window. She sat down to eat. She poured herself some Porting Wine, from Alstromia, and sipped it slowly. She started to feel a calm come over her. Suddenly, she had a brilliant idea.

Lorthana picked up Lilah and took her to the bedroom. She placed the child, still asleep, in the small crib by her bed. She pulled the warm cover over the child and walked out of the room and headed for the kitchen.

"Well, I guess someone is feeling better?" snickered Lorthana, as she watched Zandorah sipping Porting Wine. "You could have told me the food was ready, I am so hungry."

"I figured you would come into the kitchen after you put Lilah down. Yes, the wine is helping. I had an idea I want to run by you. I think I know what we need to do next."

"Okay, tell me!"

"Why don't you get some food and Porting Wine? Then, we will discuss our next step."

Lorthana happily obliged.

Meanwhile, back on Alstromia, Alexis floated over a chair in her chamber. She had her eyes closed, attempting to meditate to relieve the stress. Alexis was keenly aware of noises in the hall, making it difficult to concentrate. She was becoming increasingly annoyed. Why was everyone so darn loud, so selfish? She wanted silence! She opened her eyes and stared at the door. Suddenly, the door flew open and Aerianna entered.

"Your Majesty, I bring amazing news!" she shouted as she ran into the chamber, almost tripping over her own feet on the way in.

"Goodness, watch yourself. What are you doing?" snapped Alexis.

"Sorry, I was just so excited. I just got back from speaking with Florenzzah. I was able to negotiate for the spell. However, we may have an itsy, bitsy problem."

"Problem? What kind of problem?"

"Well, she wants more than what I was able to give her – she wants you to give her a permanent position on your royal staff." Immediately, after the words left her lips, she knew there would be trouble. Alexis would not take this news lightly. No way.

"Are you out of your mind? I am NOT giving her anything. She should be grateful we came to her, and honored I sent you. Who does she think she is? I will not be blackmailed."

"Alexis, please hear me out. Florenzzah felt our demand was higher than her payment. She wants to return to your staff. She knows you banned her because of a previous situation, however, she believes this can make you even."

"Even? Ummm, no! We are not even. Not by any means."

"Understood. However, I cannot get the spell until you agree to speak with her. Florenzzah is on her way here now. I beg you, please…give her what she asks so we can return you to normal.

Plus, Armbruster is doing whatever he wants in your absence. He is again gaining much respect. I am worried he will take the power away from you."

"For goodness sake. I am barely absent and he believes he can gain back power? I do not think so," shouted Alexis. She stood up and floated toward Aerianna. She stopped right in front of her and pointed her finger in Aerianna's direction.

"Listen! I am tired. I am sick and tired of all the games. Armbruster is not taking anything from me. As far as Florenzzah, bring her to me at once. We will negotiate, and I will deal with her later. You, get your act together. Make sure Armbruster is under control until I can get back to work. Got it?"

"Yes, Alexis. Clear. Very clear. I shall do as you command."

Aerianna turned and ran out of the chamber, slamming the door.

Alexis floated back to her chair, contemplating the previous conversation. So, Florenzzah thought she could blackmail her into gaining a royal position? Really? Not going to happen. She was well aware of Florenzzah's powers, but also knew she was not that powerful. She would show her who was boss. She would not surrender anything to a puny witch like Florenzzah. She would regret the day she attempted to blackmail her.

On Earth, Shell looked around the empty house, wondering what to do next. They had saved the child, only to lose her. She knew in her heart, she had to send word to Armbruster and tell him everything, though she feared his wrath. She also knew he would not be thrilled and most likely harm her. She was not one of his favorites. From the moment they had met, he felt a deep resentment toward her, for taking Alexis away from him. Shell's bond with Alexis was natural and good. They were soulmates, meant to meet. Armbruster did not agree. He felt it was unnatural for them to have such a bond, considering one was human and one was a witch. He had attempted to disrupt their friendship numerous times.

Shell sat on the couch in the living room and stared ahead, not saying a word. Her husband quietly sat next to her and placed his hand on hers.

"Talk to me," Joran insisted.

"No, there is nothing to say. We have to do the right thing."

"And that would be what?" he asked, with a look of fear on his face.

"You know what it is…" she replied.

"I can guess."

"I am going to send word to Armbruster. We have to tell him everything."

"Your loyalty is to Alexis, not Armbruster. I think you really need to rethink your plan, Shell," he begged.

"No. It has to be this way, trust me."

"Okay, I will not question your rationale. I am sure there are reasons why you feel this way. What can I do?"

"You can stay out of it and leave. I do not want you here when he arrives, I want you safe. I will take responsibility for what has happened. I love you."

He stood up and shook his head. "No way, I am not leaving! We are in this together, Shell. Stop this." He knew his request was futile. She would not budge. Once her mind was made up, she always followed through.

He watched as she motioned for him to leave. He nodded and walked to their bedroom to gather his belongings.

Shell stood up and walked to the fireplace. There she sat down, crossed her legs, and closed her eyes. She started thinking about Armbruster and how she would explain the situation. She heard the front door close. Joran had left, offended.

She stood up, walked to the mirror by the front door, and looked at her face. She had tears running down her cheek. Fear made her uneasy. She grabbed her jacket and walked outside, heading into town to find one of the scouts. They would know how to get ahold of Armbruster. As she walked, the wind had picked up, the cold stinging her cheeks. She wiped the wet tears away as she started to run toward town.

The council met in the Main Hall, awaiting Armbruster's arrival. There were twenty-four Guiders present, twenty-five including Armbruster, just enough to enact the Chant of Reztec. Alstromia would be secured, taking care of one problem.

The massive chamber doors opened. Armbruster, armed with numerous books, entered looking frustrated.

"Is everyone present?" he barked in a harsh tone.

Yarlen immediately stood up. "Yes, your Majesty. All present. We are ready to proceed."

"Very well. Everyone, one at a time, please introduce yourself to the others."

One by one, each Guilder stated their name, from where they originated, what their specialty was, and finally how they planned to help.

Once the introductions were complete, Yarlen instructed each Guider of their position and what was needed. The plan commenced. After what seemed like a long time, the Guiders stood in a circle with their Ceptres ready for action. Yarlen initiated the chant. Once initiated, no one could stop it. To do so, could lead to catastrophe. The Guiders became one, chanting and slamming down their powerful Ceptres. The room began to shake. Colorful swirls of light enveloped the Guiders. Yarlen giggled like a child, knowing the chant was working. It was complete. There was a loud banging and hissing noise, followed by extreme darkness. Instantly, the sky turned purple, changing the atmosphere. The planet was secure.

Armbruster smiled. The chant had worked. He walked up to each Guider and personally thanked them for their help, reassuring them their help would not be forgotten. He knew he greatly owed them all. The Guiders left, one at a time, Yarlen remained behind.

He observed Armbruster in front of a large window, admiring the purple clouds in the sky.

"Sir, we have done it."

"Yes, my friend, we have. I could not have done it without you and your team. I am forever in your debt. I promise to make it up to you one day."

"Sir, there is no need. I am only glad we were able to secure Alstromia against our enemies. What shall we do now?"

"We need to resume our hunt for my daughter. Also, I must go speak with Alexis. Please look into any news from Earth. Also, since my patience with you is dwindling, I expect you to find a way to reverse the spell on Alexis. I am tired of waiting. The time for her is running out."

"I will do so now!" Yarlen took his leave. He walked to the communication chamber to seek out what information had been received from Earth regarding the missing Princess. He was annoyed that Armbruster had remembered the need for the Reversal Spell for Alexis. He would have been fine keeping her in her current state of being. He smiled to himself, thinking it would be better not to let anyone witness his smirk. It would send the wrong message to others.

Armbruster walked to his chamber to draw up a plan, deciding to wait to see Alexis. He was not in the mood to listen to her whining. She would most likely be aggressive. Alexis had not yet been 'returned' and would be feeling vengeful. He knew Yarlen was dragging his feet about finding a reversal spell, which was why he had enlisted the help of Farla, the Great Witch, to help him. He knew Yarlen would come up with a million excuses as to why the spell could not be reversed. He was aware he had to handle the Alexis situation himself.

Alexis looked out the window, admiring the purple glow, knowing what it meant. Wow, Armbruster and Yarlen actually pulled it off, she thought. She laughed out loud and surprised herself. Sometimes, she regretted the fact she had not kept up with Armbruster and his abilities. She really had to reconsider his position, he was quite capable. She violently hated Yarlen, since it was his spell that had put her in this condition. She would make him pay. He was always so darn angry with her. It was not her fault. Armbruster always ran to Yarlen, complaining about her. It made her look incompetent. She would have a lengthy and stern conversation with Armbruster once all this all this was done and life was back to normal.

She looked over to her bed. There, her eyes caught a glimpse of the pink, sparkly blanket. She felt wetness run down her face, realizing how much she missed her precious daughter. It made her feel sick not knowing where she was, or if she was okay. She looked down at the blanked and recalled the day she had given birth. Lilah had been wrapped in that blanket, so tiny and vulnerable.

Alexis was getting angrier by the second. Her green eyes flashed with anger. At that same moment, there was a loud knock on the door.

"Your Majesty, may we enter?"

Alexis knew it was Aerianna.

"By all means, get in here," she shouted.

The door opened and Aerianna entered first, followed by Florenzzah. Aerianna walked confidently and calm toward Alexis.

"Your Majesty, I bring you Florenzzah of Tullah Mountain." She stepped back to allow Florenzzah to step forward. Florenzzah stood there, not moving. Aerianna got behind her and shoved her toward the Queen. She whispered in her ear: "don't be stupid."

"Florenzzah, step forward and come before me!" demanded Alexis.

"Your Majesty." Florenzzah bowed and lowered her head in respect.

"What have you brought me? You see my current situation. I

am not in the mood for your blackmail or your arrogance. I expect the reversal spell immediately," she hissed.

"Your Majesty. I came with the spell, but ask for a few things in return."

Alexis moved closer. "Who do you think you are, making demands to me? Are you wanting to die?" she screamed.

"Absolutely not, your Majesty…"

"Silence! Hand Aerianna the spell. Once I am returned, we will negotiate. Not until then. Do you hear me?"

"Yes, your Majesty." Florenzzah opened her large, black bag and pulled out an ancient scroll. She quickly handed it to Aerianna.

Alexis smiled. Finally, everything was about to change!

Shell walked inside and sat on the couch. She felt alone. Where was Joran? she wondered. She missed him already. She knew Armbruster would be there shortly, and there was no way to mentally prepare for that kind of a confrontation. Nevertheless, she had a plan. She was unsure how he would handle the news, but felt it needed to be done. She walked in the kitchen, poured a large glass of wine, and sat at the table waiting.

Armbruster sat behind the massive table in his chamber, looking at various updated reports from his team. As he sat reading, he heard a commanding knock on the door. He sat up and removed his glasses.

"Enter!" he yelled.

Yarlen appeared and closed the door.

"Sir, I bring news. I just heard from Senior-Scout Cinderillah. She stated Shell would like a word with you on Earth. Shell claims to have news about Princess Lilah."

Senior-Scout Cinderillah was a red-headed and feisty witch. She had volunteered to stay on Earth to be Armbruster's eyes and ears. She reported to Yarlen weekly with updates on what was happening on Earth. She was smart, and blended perfectly with the humans. She had a small team of lookouts relaying information to her. Her loyalty was to the Queen and Armbruster.

Cinderillah initiated the communication with Yarlen the minute she has received the visit from Shell, requesting to speak directly with Armbruster about the disappearance of the Princess. She knew it was important, though wondering why Shell would know anything pertaining to the kidnapping. Cinderillah had sent out her scouts to dig deeper into what Shell could possibly know. She had gotten nowhere in her quest. Frustrated, she figured it was best to contact Yarlen to inform him of this important event.

"WHAT?" Armbruster instantly stood up and walked toward Yarlen.

"What do you know?" he interrogated, eager to receive the news.

"Sir, this is the message we received."

He handed Armbruster a piece of paper. Armbruster took it and slid his glasses back on his nose. He read the note and looked off to the side, with his head slightly cocked, thinking.

The message read: *"I respectfully beg your presence. I need to speak with you, your Majesty. I have information about Lilah. I must insist your presence on Earth immediately. If you fail to show, there could be dire consequences for the Princess. – Shell"*

Armbruster looked at Yarlen.

"Have you read it?" he asked, as he pushed the note toward Yarlen and showed him the writing. He then pulled it back and held onto it tightly, like a precious gem in his hand.

"Yes, I have."

"And…what do you think?"

"Sir, my first thought was that it might be a trap. But, knowing the bond between Alexis and Shell, I must assume otherwise. I believe we need to meet and see what she knows. Would you prefer I go in your place?"

"No, we will go together. I must go. I need to hear what the human has to say. She would not have risked so much if it were not important. We must depart at once. Please, let our command staff know of our decision and get a plan in place immediately."

"Agreed. I will be back shortly with a plan." He left the chamber to find the team so they could formulate a plan to get back to Earth without being noticed.

Armbruster walked to his table and reluctantly sat down, holding the note in his left hand. He removed his glasses and cupped his face with his hands. He began to cry, his emotions too much to bare. The thought of finding out what happened to his daughter was overwhelming. The uncertainty made him feel sick to his stomach. He closed his eyes, still sobbing.

I must tell Alexis, he thought. Then it hit him. No, I will not tell her until I know more. In her current state, she will lose her mind. She will want to go to Earth, and she cannot. No one must know of her current condition. He stood up and walked to his closet to change. He knew what needed to be done and was prepared. Shell darn well better have some real news, or he would ensure her life would end. He was not in the mood to put up with her nonsense. Once and for all, she would prove her loyalty or suffer the ultimate fate.

He would return with news about Lilah, and only then, report back to Alexis. Hopefully, it would not be too late to reverse her spell. He knew Yarlen was dragging his feet on the reversal, and at this point, Armbruster did not care either. He was enjoying the revival of his power.

Aerianna and Alexis looked at the spell. It seemed too simple. How could it be? There had to be more. There was no way it was this simple. Was it a real spell, or had Florenzzah given them a fake spell? Both looked at each other smiling. Aerianna started laughing and Alexis knew they were thinking the same thing.

"She would not be that stupid, would she?" asked Alexis, a slightly amused looked on her face.

"Maybe she thinks if she gives us a fake spell or it does not work, she has more power to negotiate?"

"Well, we will see. If it does not, she will perish. I am tired of her games. I cannot believe she would be so dumb as to try to trick me. She must be crazy. We will deal with her either way. Can you get the items out of the tower? We are almost out of time."

"Yes, I can get them. I will be back shortly. You will be returned to your former self in no time, Alexis."

Aerianna left the room as quickly as she could, heading toward the tower to gather the necessary ingredients. She wanted nothing more than to quickly return Alexis to her normal state.

Alexis looked like a beautiful ghost, as she hovered above her chair. She was upright, looking ever so regal and commanding. Her face, a bit twisted, with an awkward smirk. She believed things were about to get serious. It was the calm before the storm. There was no doubt in her mind, she was going to be that the storm! She was about to regain her power! Armbruster better enjoy what little time he has left feeling in control, because it was about to stop. She was ready to step up and regain her rightful place as the Queen. No one was going to stop her this time. Yarlen was also going to pay for what he did to her. She already had a plan in place for him. Yes, she knew he had been doing everything in his power to stop the reversal spell. She was not stupid. She knew his plan, which is why she had made her own strategy. Now, her plan was almost complete. She would be in charge again. Yes, Yarlen, I am coming for you, she thought. She laughed feeling in control and very satisfied.

Yarlen and his team had a secure plan to return to Earth and question Shell. They knew time was of the essence. They met Armbruster in the Main Hall and cast a spell to return to Earth. No one knew they departed Alstromia, unaware of their plan. It was a secret rendezvous with Shell to find out what she knew about Lilah. They would find out, once and for all, if she was telling the truth. Armbruster was prepared to find out either way.

Unaware of what was going on with Armbruster, Alexis waited impatiently for Aerianna to return with the necessary ingredients to perform her Reversal Spell. She looked outside and thought about how odd it was that she was not hungry. When was the last time she had consumed food? She missed the taste of food. She missed many things. Just as her mind drifted to Lilah again, Aerianna came barging through the door, completely out of breath.

"I got it! Are you ready?" she huffed.

"Look at me! What do you think?" snapped an obviously aggravated Alexis. "So, what do we do?"

"Very simple. I have already combined everything. We simply must cast the spell in order and voila.... you will return," screeched an overly excited Aerianna.

"Alright, time is dwindling."

Seconds later, the two stood across from each other by the fireplace, all items in order. Each item was required to be poured over Alexis as the spell was being cast. Alexis started to feel warm. It was an odd, tingling sensation. She felt as if she was bathing in a hot pool of water. She smiled, as she realized she was returning. Aerianna's face reflected what Alexis felt. She could see a bright smile radiating off her friend's face.

"Alexis, you are back! You have returned!"

Alexis took her right hand and felt her body. Yes, it felt warm and normal. She looked down at her feet, admiring their fleshy color. She walked over to the full-length mirror by the bed to admire herself. I'm back, she thought, grinning from ear to ear. Without thinking, she turned around and embraced Aerianna. She felt her friend trying to pull away, feeling awkward.

"I could not have done this without you. I owe you. If it would have been up to Yarlen, I would forever be the ghostly figure. I cannot tell you how proud I am of you. I am forever grateful."

"Alexis, my Queen, it was my pleasure. It is good to see you returned. Now, let's find out what Armbruster and Yarlen are up to. Something is off, I have not seen them anywhere."

"What do you mean?"

"I mean, no one has said anything about them in a long time. I asked around to find out where they were, and what they were doing. However, even Pauto stated he had not seen either one. I think this is very strange, they must be somewhere. I can only hope all is going well with the hunt for Lilah."

"Odd indeed. We better go find out what they are up to. I will go to Armbruster's chamber to have a talk with him, should he be there. You, concentrate on finding Yarlen. He is probably still plotting to do something to keep me under his control. Whatever you do, should you find Yarlen, do not tell him of my return. I want to confront the liar myself. We both know he was never going to help me return."

"Agreed! We shall meet back here, shorty?" inquired Aerianna.

"Yes, we shall."

chapter 11

Disclosures

Yarlen, Armbruster, and their Security Command Team arrived on Earth, outside the small cottage in New England. They walked up to Cinderillah's front door and gently knocked. The curly, red-headed witch appeared by the front door.

"Your Majesty, Yarlen, please enter," she beckoned for them to enter. She led them into the living quarters of her modest cottage. She pointed to a large couch across from the fireplace.

"Please, have a seat," Cinderillah said humbly.

Armbruster and Yarlen complied and sat down. Both looked around the room. Her home was small, but cozy. The room was very simple; a small rug in the center of the room, a table, a chair, and a sofa. There was a small, standing lamp in the corner by a window. Two large candelabras stood on both sides of the fireplace.

"Sir, I am so happy you decided to come. I have been waiting to see you."

"Yes, we knew it was important. We left as soon as possible," replied Armbruster.

"Okay, we are here. Tell us what you know," said Yarlen impatiently.

"Well, I received a visit from Shell. She showed up, looking awful. She had been crying. I knew something was very wrong and I asked her to come inside. We sat in the kitchen and she told me she needed to see you. She stated she had very important information to relay. I sent out my scouts to see if they could find out anything about what she had been implying, about the kidnapping of your child. However, there was zero news. I am worried, I hope it is not a trap."

Yarlen stood up and started pacing around the room. "Yes, we had the same thought. However, given the relationship between Shell and Alexis, we do not believe it is a trap. We believe she knows something. That is why we are here." He sat back down.

"Listen, we will be heading to her home to speak with her. We wanted to see if you had any other information before we went there. I thank you for your continued loyalty and friendship. You are a great friend, Cinderillah. Alstromia is grateful." Armbruster stood up and walked toward the door, Yarlen following, Cinderillah right behind them. As Armbruster opened the door, Cinderillah spoke.

"Sir, I would love to go with you."

Armbruster spun around. "No, you have done your job. We will take care of this. You stay here and stay alert. We need you. We will be in touch."

Cinderillah bowed and thanked them. She gently closed the door.

Outside, Armbruster, Yarlen, and the Security Command Team talked for a moment about the next step. They wanted to be clear on the instructions given by Yarlen. They slammed down their Ceptres and disappeared.

Cinderillah walked to the kitchen to pour herself a large glass of Porting Wine. She was grateful Armbruster trusted and thanked her for her support. She felt proud, knowing her position on Earth was useful to the kingdom and the Queen. Somewhere in her mind, she still felt uneasy about the Shell situation and could only hope all would be okay.

Meanwhile, Armbruster, Yarlen and the Security Command

Team appeared outside Shell's home. Yarlen informed the team to secure the perimeter of the home and to be on the lookout for any suspicious activity.

Armbruster walked up to the door and knocked, cautiously looking around. Yarlen stood behind him, patiently waiting for Shell to open door. The door swung open and Shell appeared. She looked distraught and her face was flushed. She bowed, thanked them for coming, and invited them in.

Once inside, she guided them into a small sitting area off the left side of the kitchen. She meekly asked if they wanted anything to drink or eat.

"Shell, we thank you for your hospitality, but that is not why we are here. Please, tell us why you summoned us back to Earth," said an intolerant Yarlen. He looked at Shell, rolling his eyes.

"Your Majesty, Yarlen…I am afraid I have bad news. I know what happened to the Princess." She swallowed hard and tried not to look away. It was more difficult than she had anticipated. She wanted to tell them everything she knew. However, she was also afraid of their reaction.

She continued. "Sirs, Lilah was kidnapped by Loggane. He used Lilah as a means to make the Queen give him back the power he wanted. I believe, he thought it was the only way to regain what he thought was rightfully his. After he kidnapped the Princess, I was able to get the child back, with the help of Cinderillah and a few others left on Earth."

She stopped talking. She could see anger rise up in Armbruster's face.

"I wanted to protect Lilah. My main objective has been to return her to you and the Queen. It was my sole purpose to return her in a safe manner. However, before I could, someone showed up and overpowered Joran and took her out of the crib while I slept." There it was. She had told them the awful truth. She felt queasy. What was about to happen? She started to shake, but held off the tears. She knew if she started to cry, they would only feel worse and potentially see her as weak.

"What are you saying?" yelled a furious Armbruster. He looked at Shell with disgust. She had taken his daughter back from Loggane and then lost her? Who had her? His head was spinning and he was becoming angrier. Armbruster got up from the couch and lunged at Shell. He placed his hand on her shoulder and violently shook her. Her head flopped from side to side, like a broken doll. She did nothing to stop him.

"What is wrong with you, woman! What have you done?"

Yarlen got up quickly. He gently pulled Armbruster's hands away from Shell. "Sir, please," he begged.

Armbruster let go of Shell, shaking his head. He had thought he would find out where his precious daughter was being held. He had hoped to be reunited with her and to take her back to Alstromia, to Alexis. Never, had he thought Shell would have betrayed him, or Alexis.

"Shell," began Yarlen, "we need to know everything you know. Please, do not spare us any detail. We must find the Princess."

"I have told you everything I know. I have not hidden any information from you. I do not know who took her. Joran said he thought he saw a woman in a long cape, but he is not sure. Someone pushed him. He hit his head and passed out. I found him sprawled out on the floor."

"Sir, how do you want to proceed?" asked Yarlen looking at Armbruster.

Armbruster sat in silence, contemplating Shell's story. He just sat there, saying nothing, looking glum.

Shell started to talk, but decided it was best to keep quiet until Armbruster said something. She bit her bottom lip and stared ahead in silence. A few minutes passed. It seemed like an eternity to Shell.

"I believe we are done here," is all Armbruster said, as he stood up, motioning for Yarlen to walk to the door. "Shell has told us all she knows. We do not need to be wasting our time."

Shell walked behind Yarlen and Armbruster as they headed toward the front door. There, Yarlen opened the door, allowing Armbruster to exit first. He spun around on his feet to confront Shell.

"Let me be very clear, my dear. You better keep an eye out for anything on the whereabouts of the Princess. Do you understand?" he barked in her face, his eyes squinted, his finger raised at her face.

"Yes, I understand," she replied looking away, feeling like a traitor.

Yarlen touched her shoulder. "I know you meant to do the right thing. Nonetheless, we still have no idea where the Princess is, so we are back to square one. Thank you for the information." Yarlen walked outside to join Armbruster and the team. Shell had made a huge mess out of the situation. He felt it was only appropriate that he act sternly toward her.

On Alstromia, Alexis sat in front of her table. She was looking at the mirror, brushing her long, black hair. She was admiring herself, as usual. She was back to normal! She thought about the traitor, Yarlen, and smirked. She was going to make him pay for his betrayal. He would regret the day he attempted to leave her in that awful condition. She knew there was never a plan to 'return' her. She would make him pay for his disloyalty in front of Armbruster. He would witness her power and control over the situation, sending a clear message she was the only one in charge.

She finished brushing her hair and stood up. As she walked to the side of the table, she grasped her Ceptre and walked out of the room. She proceeded down the hall to find Yarlen and Armbruster. She could not wait to confront them. She would love to see their faces when they laid their eyes on her. They would die from shock alone.

Aerianna ran into Porti and started to harshly interrogate him on the whereabouts of Armbruster and Yarlen.

"I have not seen them in a while. I was looking for his Majesty to speak with him about how he wants the Command Team to proceed. We have only vague instructions on how they wish for us to conduct the search for the Princess," replied Porti.

"So, no word? That is very bizarre. I do not like it, something is wrong. Keep looking. The instant you find them, come find me. The Queen is waiting to speak with them." She nodded and walked away. More than ever before, she knew something did not feel right about the situation. What were they up to? What did they know, that she and Alexis did not? It all felt wrong. Her stomach felt peculiar, causing her to stop. She trembled lightly, but moved on. She wanted to find the two and gather more information for Alexis.

"Mom, we need to talk," started Zandorah, looking at her mother. Lorthana was holding the baby, cradled softly against her chest.

Lorthana looked up and smiled. "What is it, Zandi?"

"Mom, I got word. Shell and Joran talked to Armbruster. He knows the child was taken from them. He is hunting down the one that has his child. Mom…he is coming for us."

"We have done nothing wrong, Zandi. Calm down. We saved the child, making us heroes. He will thank us. We have nothing to worry about." She tried to reassure her daughter. Though, she felt a twinge of uncertainty about her own words.

"Excuse me…we still have Lilah, we should have returned her the chance we had. This does not look good. We need to return her before we are accused of having done this. I do not like it at all!" screeched Zandorah. She looked wild-eyed. She paced in a circle while she talked, chewing on her long, red nails.

"Stop it, Zandi. You really must calm down. You will wake the child," demanded Lorthana.

"Mom, I am concerned. I think we need to figure out how to

return Lilah. The longer we hold onto her, the more it looks like we were part of the plan. It is an awful thing."

"I agree with you, honey. I have already started the process. I have reached out, to convey a message to Armbruster. I think it is best to surrender the child to him and let him be the one to bring Lilah to Alexis. It will be done soon."

"What? What plan? Tell me more," insisted a curious Zandorah.

"Sit, my child, and listen up…"

Alexis marched down the hallway, heading for the Main Hall to confront the Security Command Team. She would grill them until someone told her where to find Armbruster and Yarlen. She was pissed off. Why had they disappeared without giving a word of their plans? How dare they keep her out of the loop!

She entered the hall to find Garlow speaking with Pauto. They saw her approach and bowed. "Your Majesty, how may we be of assistance?" asked a nervous Pauto.

"You can start by telling me where I can find my husband and Yarlen," she replied in a huff.

"Your Majesty, we do not know where they are. We were just deliberating the situation. No one has seen them in a while. Their chambers are empty; Ceptres gone."

"That is not information, Pauto. I would expect you to know their location at all times," she stated with fury.

"My Queen, I can only apologize. I promise my team is actively looking for them. I am not sure they are even still on Alstromia."

"Excuse me? Why do you assume that? Where would they be?" The second the words left her lips, she knew the answer. They had gone to Earth! Why? What was on Earth? Had they received news about Lilah? She felt her face flush. Her heart was beating so strong, she could feel it in her throat, making it difficult to swallow. She did her best to stay calm, though rage flowed through her body. She put both hands on her hips, staring at the two men.

"Get your team together and find them! I do not care where

they are. I want them found, now! Do you hear me?" Such incompetence, she thought. Why did she always have to be the one to do everything? She folded her hands and closed her eyes. Calm, stay calm, she kept telling herself.

"Yes, my Queen. It shall be done." Pauto instructed his team to get ready to depart for Earth. They would find Cinderillah and interrogate her. She always knew what was going on and would be the first stop. Everything else would have to wait until they gathered more information.

Alexis turned her back on Pauto and Garlow and headed back to her chamber. She hoped Aerianna would be waiting with some new developments. During the long walk to her chamber, she contemplated what Yarlen and Armbruster could be doing. She was getting angrier with each step she took. She preferred to walk, rather than use magic to transport herself. It allowed her to clear her head, giving her time to think in peace, without interruptions.

Aerianna opened the chamber door, looking for Alexis. She was not back; the chamber was empty. What should she do? Just as she was about to leave, Alexis entered the room looking obviously agitated. Her face was red, her hair looked messy, and she had a scowl on her face as though she wanted to kill someone.

"There you are," she said to Aerianna. "What did you find out?"

"Nothing! No one knows anything. It is as if they both just disappeared. I don't believe they are here on Alstromia. I believe they are on Earth."

"Yes, I agree. I spoke with Pauto and Garlow, they feel the same. They are on their way now to hunt them down. I would like to know what they are doing on Earth. I am frankly shocked that they kept me out their plans. They should have known I would be less than pleased once I got wind of their deceptiveness. Wait and see, Aerianna. They will be sorry. I cannot tell you how tired I am of all this nonsense. The constant lies and deceit. It is getting old."

"What shall we do now, Alexis?"

"Nothing, we must wait. I have to put a plan together to confront Yarlen, take back my rightful power, and find my daughter. I will stay in my chamber. You, get out there and keep looking. I expect a report back later tonight. I do not wish to be disturbed, unless you have something useful to say. Okay?"

"Yes, your Majesty. Enjoy your rest."

"Rest? What is wrong with you? I am not going to rest. Next time, think about what you are about to say, before you say it. Stupid girl. You are dismissed," she waived her hands, indicating she was discharging Aerianna. Aerianna got the message and left quickly. Alexis was definitely upset. It was best, under the circumstance, to stay out of her way.

Alexis sat on the edge of her bed, staring at the fireplace. The Trimbers burned, cracking, producing a green and purple glow. She loved the fire. Where was Armbruster? He better be on his way back with some useful information, she thought. She subconsciously kicked her feet, as she sat mesmerized by the flames dancing in the fireplace. Nothing made sense. She felt tired and wanted to sleep. However, she knew there was no way she would be able to, even if she tried. Instead, she decided to sit and wait. Someone would bring her some information, it was just a matter of time.

On Earth, the team had decided to head back to Alstromia. There was no reason to stay on Earth, having reached a dead end in attempting to find the Princess. Once back in the Main Hall, in the Palace, Armbruster stared at Yarlen, with a look of defeat on his face. The team remained quiet, awaiting further instructions. The trip to Earth had not been very helpful in finding the Princess. Armbruster felt at a loss. He had no idea what to do and knew Yarlen felt the same. He could see it on his face. Everyone looked exhausted.

Armbruster spoke up. "I will go and update the Queen. She must be informed of what we have found out." He knew the conversation would not go well. However, not telling Alexis right away would only infuriate her more. As soon as she found out he had been hiding something from her, it would be much worse.

Yarlen grabbed Armbruster's sleeve. "Sir, I do not think that is a wise choice, considering the Queen's current condition," he added, thinking about Alexis in her permanent, ghostly state. He tried desperately to hide his smile.

"No, she must be informed. I will go." He pushed himself away from the table and got up. He left the room to find Alexis. Yarlen stayed behind to speak with his team, instructing them on what needed to be done next. He wondered what would happen when Alexis realized she was permanently a ghostly figure. A wave of fear ripped through him. He realized he was in trouble. Alexis would blame him. She would hold him accountable and most likely, kill him.

Armbruster approached the door, apprehensively. First, how would Alexis feel, knowing her state was now forever permanent? They had failed to reverse her condition. She would be outraged. Second, how would she react to all the new information he had gathered on Earth? Third, would she be upset once he told her about Shell? He knew it had to be done. He pushed open the door to confront Alexis.

Alexis sat quietly, still kicking her feet, staring at the fireplace when Armbruster plowed through the door.

The instant he saw her, in her reinstated glory, came to an abrupt stop. He stared, in disbelief. What happened? he thought. She could see his perplexed look. She laughed, nodding her head.

"What? You thought I would leave my fate up to you and that worthless, Second in Command, Yarlen?" she cackled. "No way. I knew, the only way I would be returned is if I put Aerianna in charge. That girl… she is better than I thought. Close your mouth, Armbruster. It is not a very attractive sight."

"But, but…. how?"

"Quite simply. My capable friend and confidant, conducted

some research. She found someone with a reversal spell. She brought her to me, we got the reversal spell from her, and there you have it. The rest is history," she proclaimed proudly. She knew he was shocked and she loved it! Nothing better than catching them off guard, she thought.

"Honey, I am so happy," proclaimed Armbruster as he approached to hug her.

"Stop it. You do not care either way, it was apparent by your look. You expected me to still be the ghostly figure you left. You, as always, underestimate me and Aerianna. You really need to get your stuff together, Armbruster. I am shocked at your disregard for me and my well-being." She stood up and walked toward him. Looking him right in the face, she slapped him hard across his right cheek. Shocked, all he could do was look at her. "You are not the man I married. Where is your loyalty? I hope you enjoyed your little time in charge. It will end now. Get out of here and bring me Yarlen, I have a few things to discuss with your traitorous friend."

"Alexis…." he started to say, rubbing is throbbing cheek. "I have news. I need to speak with you."

"Unless you know where my child is, we have nothing to say. You are dismissed." She pointed to the chamber door.

"No, you have to hear this. Sit down!" he insisted.

Intrigued, she sat down and looked up at him with her piercing, green eyes. He felt a wave of heat rush through him. He was scared. How to start? He decided he would start at the beginning.

After a few minutes of recounting every detail, he sat down in the chair by the fireplace next to her, awaiting her reaction. She looked stunned. There was no response. He had expected her to yell, scream, throw something, do something. But, nothing. She stared ahead at the fireplace, quietly. This was bad. She was never quiet. Quiet was terrifying. Obviously, something was about to happen.

chapter 12

Confrontations

Alexis slammed down her Ceptre in anger. Instantly, she appeared before Shell's house. She pounded on the door. Quickly, the door opened, a stunned Shell looked her in the face. Her eyes bugged out. Her body instantly felt like jelly.

"Alexis..." she said quietly, looking down.

"Well, are you going to let me in, or what?"

"Of course! Please, come in." Shell gestured for her to enter the house. Once inside, Alexis stood in the entryway, facing Shell.

"So, exactly when were you going to tell me? Did you really think I would not find out?"

"Alexis, let me explain!" begged Shell.

"STOP IT. Stop with the lies, I've had enough. I trusted you!"

"Alexis, everything I did, I did for you. I wanted to protect Lilah. I never meant to hurt you. You must believe me. I would not lie to you."

"Sure, I believe you.... not." retorted Alexis.

"Listen, I knew you would be upset. I felt it was best to tell Armbruster first. I figured it would be better if he could smooth things over and explain everything to you."

"Oh, did you now?"

"Well, it seemed the right plan, at the time. Alexis, I really did think I was doing the right thing. I promise."

Alexis watched, as Shell stood across from her, looking terrified. She waited for more of an explanation to follow her comment.

"I knew you would want to know, but I was afraid of your reaction. I messed up. I am very sorry. Please…forgive me." She started to cry. The emotions overtook her. Alexis remained firm in her stance, not caring about her fake tears. She wanted to hug her and tell her it was okay, but at the same time, she felt blindsided. She allowed Shell to cry. Alexis continued to watch without saying a word, sending a clear message. She had been betrayed by her best friend.

Shell stopped crying and wiped her tears. She looked up at Alexis with an apologetic smile.

"Please, say something. Anything," she insisted.

"Exactly what do you expect me to say? You betrayed me? You hurt me? You're a hypocrite? I don't know what you want," hissed Alexis.

"I deserve that! However, my loyalty has always been to you. You know that."

Alexis pondered her words. "Yes, I suppose so. I guess, I can admit you did the right thing, but in a very twisted and wrong way." Alexis would not admit she was wrong. She did not admit her faults, especially to a human, no matter what a good friend she was.

"Come, sit down. Let us talk. I will tell you everything," said Shell.

The two sat down and began a lengthy conversation. Alexis felt at ease. Why was it so easy and natural to be here with Shell? Never any expectations, no demands. Shell was still one of the best things in her life, and she knew it. The two talked and talked. They even laughed, here and there. The friendship was still there. They both felt it.

Armbruster and Yarlen decided enough time had passed. They would need to find out who had kidnapped Lilah. This nightmare would need to come to an end. Armbruster looked at Yarlen and smiled. Yarlen knew what he was about to say.

"Lorthana!" the two said in unison.

"Indeed, my friend. We must head to Iriss and see her immediately. She has the baby, I feel it."

"Agreed. I shall get our Security Command Team ready." Yarlen went to find the team and make plans for their immediate departure.

Armbruster entered the chamber, looking for Alexis. She was not in her room.

It made him want to find Aerianna and make her divulge where Alexis had gone. He found Aerianna in her chamber and he began his interrogation. "Where is she?" he demanded. Aerianna looked at him confused, shrugging her shoulders.

"What are you talking about, your Majesty?"

"I want to know where I can find my wife. You know where to find her. Where is she?" Armbruster grew impatient. Why was Aerianna pretending she did not know where to find Alexis?

"Sir, last time I saw her, she was in her chamber. I left her there a while ago. Are you sure she is not there?"

"No, she is not. Very well, I will find her on my own. If you see her, tell her I know where Lilah may be. Tell her I am off to see Lorthana."

He stormed out of the room, heading to the Main Hall to retrieve his team and depart Alstromia.

Alexis and Shell said their goodbye's. Alexis nodded in approval, as she slammed down the Ceptre, returning to Alstromia. Instantaneously, she stood in her chamber, with a triumphant grin on her face. She knew where to find Lilah – Lorthana and Zandorah had her. Why though? She could not understand why they would have taken her baby. Was Zandorah threatened by the baby, or was she jealous? Why would she stoop so low as to kidnap her child? She was confident all answers would be revealed soon.

Wait until they see me, she thought. They will regret the day they took Lilah.

Aerianna entered the chamber and found Alexis sitting quietly in her chair. She knew that was not a good sign. She approached without saying a word.

Alexis watched as Aerianna approached.

"What is it now?" she said with obvious annoyance.

"Your Majesty, I have news. Armbruster just told me he knows where we can find Lilah."

"That is not news, I already know. She is on Iriss with my mom and sister."

"How do you know this?" asked a stunned Aerianna. How did Alexis always know things before she did?

"I am not stupid. I can figure these things out myself. I do not need idiots to relay information to me."

"Of course, my Queen."

"So, now…get your stuff together, we are heading to Iriss to collect Lilah and find out why these women thought for one second they could kidnap my child."

Armbruster and his team arrived outside Zandorah's home. Armbruster knocked on the door, waiting. No one came to the door. He knocked again, louder this time.

Lorthana opened the door, not looking surprised.

"We've been expecting you," she simply said.

"I would think so," replied Armbruster, pushing her aside, forcing his way past her.

His security team and Yarlen followed.

Inside the home, he stopped to stare at Lorthana. She had a blank look on her face and did not move.

"I honestly did not know if you would show up, I was worried it would be Alexis. I really was hoping it would be you as I wanted time to explain before she arrived. We both know she will come."

"Yes, you are better off explaining it to me. I will not end your life, but Alexis may!"

"Sir, I never intended to do anything to hurt either of you. In fact, Zandorah and I took the child from Shell to ensure her safety. Shell retrieved the child from Loggane. So, you see, we sort of worked together to save the child," she rationalized to Armbruster, hoping he would buy her story.

"I see. So, you're the hero in all this?"

"Not really, simply a loyal member of your family protecting you and my grandchild. That is all."

"And Zandorah? Where is she?"

"She is in the other room with the child. I asked her to watch her while I answered the door."

"I want to see my child, right now. Go get her. Also, bring Zandorah with you," demanded Armbruster. The veins in his head poking out in anger. He had enough.

"Yes, I will do so now. Please wait here," she scurried off.

Armbruster stood by the entry waiting for Zandorah, Lorthana, and Lilah to appear. Just as he was about to complain to Yarlen, he heard yelling outside. He instructed Yarlen to find out what was going on.

Yarlen did not come back. Instead, Alexis appeared with Aerianna. Her smug face told him all he needed to know – she had figured it out. How was she always only one step behind him?

"There you are, my lovie," she sarcastically said, looking at Armbruster. "Where is my child and the two worthless witches?"

"They will be right here. Lorthana went to retrieve Lilah and Zandorah." There was nothing else he could say, she already knew, or she would not have come. He rolled his eyes at her. She instantly noticed.

"What, you did not think I knew? How stupid do you think I am? You completely underestimate me and those loyal to me, Armbruster. When are you going to learn? I am still in control."

"I never thought you were stupid, Alexis. I wanted to protect you. It was my intention to bring you our child. All would have been back to normal," he explained.

She put up her hand, signaling for him to stop talking.

"Blah, blah, blah…stop talking. I hear the words, but they mean little. You did not trust me with the truth. We obviously have bigger problems."

Lorthana advanced, holding Lilah. Zandorah was right behind her, as if hiding.

Alexis walked over and ripped the baby out of Lorthana's arms.

"How dare you?" she hissed at her mother. "How dare both of you?" she shouted, looking directly at her sister.

"Alexis…" started Lorthana. She stopped, knowing anything she says would be futile. Alexis would make her own conclusions, anyways. There would be no talking to her, simply wasted breath.

Zandorah stayed behind Lorthana, not saying a word. She knew this was a horrible situation. She valued her existence and decided to keep her big mouth shut.

Alexis gently kissed the child on the cheek and smiled, then handed Armbruster the baby.

Once Lilah was safely in Armbruster's arms, Alexis walked up to Zandorah.

"So, sis, what have you got to say for yourself?"

"Nothing. I have nothing to say, Mom already said all. I love you, Alexis. I have always been there for you and always will be.

To everyone's surprise, Alexis walked up to Zandorah, grabbed and embraced her.

Lorthana, Aerianna, and Armbruster looked perplexed. This was not the reaction they had expected.

"I know, Zandi. I know," Alexis whispered, embracing her sister.

The two started crying, another first for them. The room remained silent, as the others looked on in utter shock. The group stayed in the living room and spent a long time talking. The baby slept quietly in her mother's arms.

Alexis stood up and announced their departure. Zandorah and Lorthana proceeded to say their goodbyes, still shocked at the outcome. Aerianna looked at Alexis, completely confused. There was no way Alexis would be so forgiving and kind to Zandorah. It had to be a game or plan.

Alexis and Aerianna arrived at the Palace and sat on the landing deck. Both remained silent for a while. Aerianna finally spoke. It was killing her. She needed to know why Alexis was pretending all was okay with Zandorah. She knew Alexis and was aware of her hatred for her sister.

Alexis watched the water dance in the fountain. She smiled, feeling good. She smiled at Aerianna, but said nothing. Alexis continue to watch the water, then closed her eyes. She thought about how everything had worked out in her favor. Nothing was going to stop her. She always had an ulterior motive.

Aerianna observed Alexis, wondering why she remained silent. The evening was perfect. The breeze, warmer than usual, the sky clear. Aerianna couldn't stand it any longer.

"Alexis, your Majesty, I must know…why did you embrace Zandorah? I know it is none of my business, however, there is no way after everything that has transpired, you are okay with all of it?"

"Aerianna, there is a reason you are my Second in Command. You know me all too well," snickered Alexis with a huge grin.

"So, will you tell me why?"

"Zandorah and I will never be okay, she broke my heart. She betrayed me. I can play the game just like everyone else. Yes, I could have been harsh. I could have made a scene in front of my family, but why? This is much better for all. My mother would have been heartbroken. I do not need more drama in my life."

"I see, Alexis."

"Do you? I will deal with Zandorah some other time. For now, let's just say, we are even. I have more pressing issues to contend with…"

"Now what?" questioned Aerianna, as she watched Alexis. She knew Alexis was not ready to share her plan. It was in her best interest to act concerned, but not bossy or nosy. It would only infuriate Alexis.

"Aerianna, we will discuss this further at another time. For now, we must focus on Armbruster, Yarlen, and the celebration. My child is back, we have much to do. I want to focus on the positive for a change." Alexis smiled, attempting to look sincere.

"Yes, you are correct, Alexis. We shall focus on better things and put Zandorah on the back burner, until you are ready to deal with the situation."

"Deal with the situation? I am ready to deal with it now, this just isn't the time. We will make a move when I am ready, not before. Understood?" Alexis explained, shaking her head.

"Of course, my Queen. I will be ready to come to your aid when you are ready. Shall we proceed with the celebration planning?" Aerianna asked, hoping to avoid a confrontation with Alexis. She knew deflection was key. It was always better to stay in good graces with Alexis.

"Yes, let us focus on the celebration. However, we still will need to discuss Yarlen and his betrayal. I will be addressing his disloyalty and will make him pay."

"Of course, my Queen. I understand. Please, tell me how I may be of assistance."

"I never thought you'd ask…"

Lorthana and Zandorah stared at each other in disbelief. Why had it been so easy? Why was Alexis suddenly so forgiving?

"Mom, I do not understand. I cannot believe Alexis would let go of her hatred for me so easily. Do you really believe she has forgiven me? Can we really move on?" Zandorah remained skeptical.

"Child, I believe in miracles. Alexis has not always been cold-hearted. There was a time when she was loving and kind. She loves you. Do not overthink the situation." Lorthana wanted to believe Alexis had reacted the way she did in order to make peace.

"I hope you are right, Mom. I am just completely shocked."

Gardone entered the kitchen and smiled at his wife and daughter.

"What are you two talking about," he asked.

"We were discussing today's events. It is a long story. I hope you have some time," answered Lorthana with a smirk on her face.

"Oh, do tell, Hana," Gardone responded.

"I will, dear, at a later time. Where have you been? I was getting worried."

"I have been busy. Meetings with my team. Nothing for you to worry about, dear."

"Okay, Gardone. I understand." Lorthana felt he was keeping something from her, how evasive he was his answer. However, she did not want to focus on that. She wanted to enjoy the moment. For now, her family was happy. Things had turned out better than expected and was not going to let Gardone ruin it for her.

Once back on Alstromia, Armbruster instructed the Guiders to remove the Chant and give the all clear. The child was back and everyone was safe, there was no need for the protection chant anymore.

Armbruster sat in Visitation Hall with his Security Team to discuss Collan's death. They had come to the conclusion, that he was an unfortunate victim of circumstance. He had witnessed Loggane and his team enter Alstromia and had been murdered, to keep silent. It allowed them to kidnap the child, and escape with enough time to make it back to Earth.

Armbruster would update Essten and Marittaz. He would also ensure they would never have to worry about feeding their family.

Essten's family had paid the ultimate price for their loyalty to the Queen and Alstromia.

Alexis left the landing deck, to hurry back to Lilah. She wanted to spend time with her child and enjoy her safe return. When she finally stood over the baby's crib, Alexis smiled down at her, her heart melting. It made her realize, Lilah was the only good thing to happen to her in a very long time. No wonder Loggane had used her as a weapon to attempt blackmail. Alexis smiled. He had lost that battle, she had taken care of him. She had won. She picked up Lilah and held her tight. Alexis walked to the window and looked out, turning Lilah around so the baby would face the window.

"Look, my precious. This is now your kingdom. One day, you will rule it. I will guide you and teach you well. You will never have to worry about anything again." She smiled, as the baby let out a small sigh, as if she had understood her mother. Alexis felt proud. She felt confident her baby would become a powerful Queen one day. She held Lilah for a while, not wanting the moment to end. She gently played with her tiny fingers, looking at the child with pure adoration.

Alexis handed Lilah to Carmin and instructed her to bathe the child and put her back in the crib. It had been a long time since Alexis felt this good. There was just one final step she had to complete – to deal with Yarlen and his ultimate betrayal.

chapter 13

Getting Even

Alexis and Aerianna had a plan. It was simple, quick, and exactly the point they wanted to make. They planned an elaborate Welcome Home celebration for Lilah and her triumphant, safe return. During the celebration, Alexis would put her final plan in play. Yarlen would pay for his betrayal, once and for all.

The invitations had been sent, the RSVPs received, and all was ready. The party was about to start. The Security Team was in place, the mood was cheerful, and Alexis smiled, knowing she was about to take back all of her power.

The room was filled with an enormous crowd and the food was on the tables. There was laughter, creating a joyous atmosphere. Aerianna smiled as she looked over at Alexis. Here we go again, Aerianna thought.

Once again, Armbruster sat quietly next to Alexis, clueless about what was about to happen. Yarlen sat next to him, smiling at the crowd, unaware of what was about to take place.

Aerianna stood. "Ladies and Gentlemen, please be silent! Our Queen has an announcement to make. I ask you to remain silent as she speaks." She sat down next to Alexis and nodded.   Alexis smirked and stood up behind the table. She placed the palms of her hands firmly on the table, pushing her body forward. She looked at the crowd, expressionless.

"Everyone, thank you so much for coming out to welcome back my beautiful daughter! We are so happy and relieved she is home safe. As you have probably heard by now, Loggane attempted to overtake our kingdom, using my child as his weapon of choice. He did not succeed. I ended his worthless and traitorous life. He left me with no choice." She continued. "Furthermore, we have another among us who also thought he could betray me and get away with it. This, I assure you, will never happen. I am not stupid nor blind. I have many loyal clan members on my staff, I know everything." She motioned for her Security Team to approach. They walked up behind Yarlen, waiting for further instruction from Alexis. Armbruster watched, looking completely confused and caught off-guard.

"Yarlen, you have betrayed me. I know what you were planning," she hissed. "I will not go into details here, we will discuss it at your trial. Frankly, I am shocked you felt the need to betray me. You are hereby charged with treason and will be exiled to the High Tower until your trial. Security, take him away!" She smiled, with an evil grin on her face.

Finally, Yarlen would know what it meant to have betrayed her. He would be forced to think about his actions as he sat alone, in the High Tower, with little hope of ever experiencing freedom.

The crowd watched as the Command Security Team leader, Pauto, snagged Yarlen's Ceptre from his hand. Yarlen released it without a fight. Next, Pauto grabbed him by the scruff of his neck and guided him toward the door. Yarlen managed to turn around briefly, to look Alexis in the eyes. She turned her head away and ignored him. "Get moving, Yarlen…" instructed Pauto, as he shoved Yarlen through the door, out of the Hall. Once Yarlen and the Security Command Team left, Alexis made her next announcement.

"So, now that the unpleasant part of the evening is complete, please… everyone, enjoy! Let us celebrate why we are here. Have fun." She clapped, beaming with an obvious, self-righteous look on her face. Aerianna stood up and clapped as well, showing her support for Alexis. Before too long, the entire room was filled with clapping witches and warlocks. The only one not clapping was Armbruster.

Armbruster sat, head down, shaking his head, feeling overwhelmed. He knew Alexis would do something about Yarlen, but he never thought she would throw him in the High Tower or charge him with treason. Armbruster knew his loyalty to Yarlen would have to cease immediately. He would not be able to stay loyal to his friend and wife at the same time. She would not tolerate that and would view it as betrayal. He did not want the drama nor the heartache. He decided it was best to leave Yarlen in the High Tower for now, without any form of communication.

The trial would be the deciding factor, whether he would maintain his friendship with Yarlen. His heart felt heavy. Part of him felt guilty. He had not stood up for Yarlen, nor attempted to save him. However, he knew it would have been a moot point. Alexis would have completed her plan, regardless. He was no longer in control. She had expeditiously completed her plan and regained her power…in one very decisive move.

The evening came to an end. The visitors departed, and the clean-up crew worked hard to get the palace back into its former glory. They had their orders to ensure all was done before the morning. The Queen did not like it when there was too much commotion going on.

Off in the High Tower, Yarlen sat on a very uncomfortable cot, looking out at the sky through his underwhelming, round window. He knew Alexis would not end his life. Rather, she would ensure he lived to suffer a drawn-out and awful life. He made a huge mistake, thinking he was being loyal to Armbruster. Armbruster had not yet come to see him, a clear indication he was siding with his wife. Yarlen was on his own.

There would be a trial. A very one-sided trial, for sure. There was no chance he would not be found guilty. If found guilty, he could be stripped of all his magic, his weapons, and remanded to the High Tower for eternity. Worse, he could be returned to Earth. There, life would be useless without his power. He knew either way, he was doomed. He had placed his loyalty with someone he trusted, only to have the trust broken. Yarlen became angry. He stood up and stretched. He knew he would need to find an ally, someone clever, inconspicuous, and completely unexpected. He pondered the possibilities. Suddenly, he smiled. He knew who it should be. There was no doubt she would do it, she would want revenge as much as Yarlen. She knew what it felt like to be betrayed.

Alexis stood next to her chamber's fireplace watching the flames flicker, looking smug. All had worked out the way she wanted and planned. Her strategy had been flawless, as usual. However, there was a slight twinge of something not right. She attempted to shake it off. She paced back and forth, still feeling uneasy. Why was she feeling this uncertainty? What could possibly be wrong? The evening had been fantastic, her plan perfect.

Armbruster entered her chamber and approached Alexis. Before she could say anything, he pulled her close and kissed her softly. He ran his fingers through her thick, black hair. He loved this crazy witch. He admired her, even though at times, she was one of the most infuriating beings he had ever known. Yet, he knew it was part of the appeal. It was what drew him close to her. Armbruster was delighted things seemed to be returning to normal. Perhaps now, they would be able to move forward and make their kingdom strong and powerful, the way they had both planned.

For the first time, in a long time, Alexis did not resist his kiss, instead, she reciprocated. Waking up the morning, she stretched and looked at Armbruster. He was deeply sleeping and lightly snoring, curled up on his side, facing her. He looked peaceful.

The blanket was pulled up to his nose, only exposing his eyes and forehead. He looked warm and cozy.

She rolled off the edge of the bed and pulled back the heavy blanket. Alexis jumped out of bed and walked swiftly across the cold chamber, feeling the icy floor beneath her bare feet. She pulled back the doors of the wardrobe closet, impatiently searching for her favorite robe. Once she found it, she dressed in a hurry. She stared at the mirror, tapping her finger on her lip, as she reminisced about the previous night's events, beaming with delight.

Alexis approached Aerianna's chamber and without knocking pushed open the creaking, heavy door. Across the room, she spotted Aerianna sitting on her bed. She looked pale, white as a ghost, fidgeting with the sleeve of her robe. Aerianna looked up, obviously deep in thought, her eyes glazed over. She looked at Alexis, contemplating the bad news she was about to share.

"Aerianna, what is wrong? Everything worked out as we had planned. We had a remarkable evening. Why do you look like that? What is going on?" Alexis stared at Aerianna, impatiently waiting for her response.

"I do not know how to tell you this, but we have a problem. A very, very, big problem! You are not going to like it, not one bit!"

"What are you saying? Speak up, you stupid girl. I am not in the mood for guessing games."

"Alexis, you better sit down. This is going to take a while……"

THE END…. or is it?

CPSIA information can be obtained
at www.ICGtesting.com
Printed in the USA
LVHW041023161019
634268LV00002B/381/P